ROMANCE WITH A SIDE OF GREEN CHILE

MARCIA LYNN McCLURE

Published by Distractions Ink
1290 Mirador Loop N.E.
Rio Rancho, NM 87144

Published by Distractions Ink
©Copyright 2017 by M. Meyers
A.K.A. Marcia Lynn McClure
Cover Photography by © Bambi L. Dingman/Dreamstime.com
and © Gotstock/Dreamstime.com
Cover Design and Interior Graphics by Sandy Ann Allred/Timeless Allure

First Printed Edition: March 2017

McClure, Marcia Lynn, 1965—
Romance with a Side of Green Chile: a novella/by Marcia Lynn McClure.

ISBN: 978-0-9980595-7-0

Library of Congress Control Number: 2016953226

Printed in the United States of America

To Amy L.C.L. and Bobbie L.T.D.—My Vatas!
For our beloved childhood-to-adult years together
in the beautiful Land of Enchantment—
For all our adventures, and so many wonderful memories—
Too many to list, but never too many to remember and cherish!
I love you both more than you'll ever know,
my treasured Burqueñas BFFs!

Glossary

Burqueños | plural noun | [burr-KYEN-nyos]: (1) Those who are native to Albuquerque, New Mexico, or (2) the language, including colloquialisms, common to natives of Albuquerque, New Mexico.

Cata | name | [CAW-tuh]: Spanish female name, variance of or short for Catalina.

Eee | exclamation | [Eeeee]: Wow! Oh no! Yikes! Eek!

Híjole | exclamation | [EEE-hoe-lay]: Wow! Oh no! Yikes! Eek!

Hui | exclamation | [OOO-weee]: Oh no! or Ouch!

Órale | interjection | [OH-rrrah-lay, often sounding as OH-dah-lay]: Hello! What's up? That's amazing! I agree with you! I'm flabbergasted! Hurry up! I'm waiting for you! Watch out! What's taking you so long? You're kidding me! No way! Bring it on! How funny! Wait up! Go ahead—make my day!

Ombers | interjection | [om-BERS]: Used to playfully express, Tsk tsk tsk! Shame on you!

Ruger | proper noun | [ROO-grrr]: American-based firearms manufacturing company.

Querida | term of endearment | [keh-RRREE-dah]: My darling.

Sopapilla | noun | [so-puh-PEE-yah]: A puffy, deep-fried Mexican pastry, served with honey in New Mexico.

Que no | term of inquiry | [keh-NO]: Spanish or Burqueño inquiry of validation, meaning, Am I right? or I'm right, right?

Vato/Vata | slang term | [VAH-toe or VAH-tah]: Spanish, Mexican, Hispanic, or New Mexican slang meaning dude or guy.

Villarreal | surname | [viya-rrray-AL]: A Spanish, Mexican, Hispanic, or New Mexican surname.

CHAPTER ONE

"Hey, Talli!" Cata greeted as Talli handed Cata the parking voucher. "I was hoping I'd see you this morning."

"Hey, Cata," Talli said, delighted to see her I-only-see-you-once-a-year friend, Cata Armijo. "What's the wind like today?"

"Seven miles per hour. So far, so good," Cata answered. "If it holds like this for the next couple of hours, they oughta launch with no problem."

"I'll keep my fingers crossed then," Talli promised. "Do I park in the same area this year?"

"Yep," Cata affirmed. "Just turn left here, and then head on over to the vendor parking," she added, motioning to her left with her red-glowing traffic baton. "I'll be sure to come see you before I leave. Gotta start the fiesta off with my annual funnel cake binge, huh?"

Talli giggled, "Oh yeah! I gain five pounds every year working the fiesta. It's ridiculous!"

Cata laughed and stepped back from Talli's car so that she could drive on. "We have to have lunch a couple of times this week, girl! Breakfast burritos, que no?"

"Villarreal's breakfast burritos, for reals!" Talli laughed. "I'll see you later, Cata. Good luck parking five trillion people this morning."

"Thanks! You be sure to have a great morning," Cata called as Talli turned left and headed for the vendor parking area.

After parking, Talli stepped out into the cool, crisp air of a refreshing Albuquerque morning. Making sure she had everything she needed—her jacket, backpack, extra frying apron—Talli locked her red Ford Focus with her key fob and then stood there in the vendor's parking area for a long, peaceful moment. It never failed— never. Each year, the beauty and wonder of the Albuquerque International Balloon Fiesta never failed to cause Talli's heart to swell with excitement. Furthermore, as corny as it might sound to some, to Talli, her soul never felt more cognizant, more free, more joyous in simply being alive than in October—especially for the nine glorious, crisp and cool, perfect autumn-in-New-Mexico mornings when a six-hundred-plus kaleidoscope of hot air balloons from all over the world gathered to ascend into the brilliant azure of the Albuquerque sky!

It was exactly why Talli paused before heading into the balloon park—for the fact that there were only nine days a year that felt so filled with chilled, fresh silence and the breathtaking sense that something extraordinarily rare was about to take place.

"Ahhhh," Talli breathed. "There you are," she whispered to October. The food bouquet that scented the air of the balloon fiesta was slight as yet, for at four a.m. the food vendors stretching a third of a mile along the east perimeter of the balloon field had only just begun to heat their oil, fry their bacon and sausage, and warm their tortillas in preparation of the mass assembly of spectators that would begin descending on the field by five a.m.

"There you are, my beloved October," Talli whispered again. She did not rush—did not hurry down to the field right away. Nope. She was going to enjoy every moment of October and the fiesta, just as she had every year for as long as she could remember.

The sudden, though light, aroma of hot chocolate passed over her for just an instant. And it was only an instant. Yet that instant was long enough to send Talli's mind reeling back to cherished memories of her childhood—of sitting in the back of her father's pickup, drinking hot chocolate from her My Little Pony thermos, and nibbling on a cold cinnamon Pop-Tart, an apple, and maybe a bagel with cream cheese—or whatever else her mother had so quickly and so lovingly tossed into her matching My Little Pony lunch box—comfortably bundled up in her pajamas, bunny slippers, and flannel quilt her grandmother had made. Yep, those were the balloon fiestas of her childhood, the ones she still adored most—when her dad and mom would wake Talli and her two older brothers up before the sun had risen, bundle them up warm and cozy, drive out to the then-undeveloped area of Albuquerque's North Valley, and sit in the bed of the pickup eating a terrible but delicious breakfast as the family watched the balloons launch from the balloon field—watched them drift overhead, sometimes coming so close they could wave and exchange, "Good morning!" with the balloonists.

Then, after an hour or so, Talli's parents would drive the short trip home, see that Talli and her brothers had a good drink of water and a quick trip to the bathroom, then tuck them snug as bugs back into their soft comfortable beds, and let them sleep until they woke to the bright morning sun, wondering for just an instant if the rainbow of hot air balloons floating overhead had been only a dream. Those were the balloon fiestas of her young childhood; those were her precious memories that in that moment brought tears of nostalgia to her eyes and yet soothed her heart at the same time.

Inhaling deeply, Talli opened her eyes then, gazing up into the dark four a.m. sky and smiling as several stars seemed to wink at her alone. "There you are, October," Talli whispered to the stars.

Exhaling a sigh of contentment, Talli started toward the park entrance. She smiled when she saw a man and woman nearby whom she recognized as the kettle corn vendors.

"Good morning," she said quietly.

"Good morning," the man greeted.

"Good morning," the woman said. "Feels like we might have a good first day so far."

"It sure does," Talli agreed with a smile.

That very second, the adored, distinctive scent of roasted green chile wafted through the air, and Talli's smile broadened when she heard the kettle corn couple exclaim, "Mmmm!" in unison with her own voice.

All three laughed, albeit quietly, exchanging smiles and nods once more, and Talli marveled at the fact that, even for the excitement of the upcoming events of the day—even for the fact that noise, emotion, color, and overeating would draw every visitor and worker at the park into excited chatter and talk—the still-dark hours of a balloon fiesta morning found everyone talking quietly, almost in whispers. Talli used to think that it was simply because everyone was so tired. Vendors arrived hours before the balloonists, after all— hours before those visitors from every corner of the world who had come to enjoy the event. Still, as she'd grown up and older, and especially after she'd begun working at the funnel cake stand, she'd begun to realize the quiet conversations and comments, the almost-whispered greetings, were in truth spurred by a shared sort of devoted awe that everyone experienced. Whether vendor, balloonist, or visitor, everyone stood in wonderment at the phenomenon—each and every year.

"Good morning, officer," Talli greeted an Albuquerque policeman at the front gate.

"Morning," the rugged LEO said with a smile. "Looks like they'll fly today…at least so far, hmmm?"

"It sure does," Talli agreed. "Have a good day!"

"You too, ma'am," the policeman said with a nod.

As Talli walked down the steep incline leading from the parking lot to the field, she inhaled another deep breath. The sensational aromas of scrumptious breakfast burritos descended over her all at once.

"Mmm!" she moaned to herself. As soon as her favorite breakfast burrito vendor was open for business, she would snatch one of those yummies up as quickly as she could!

Of course, thinking about breakfast burritos again brought to Talli's mind her favorite breakfast burrito vendor, Villarreal's. And thinking of Villarreal's instantly sent her hoping that the hot, mysterious Villarreal's employee from the past five years running would again be working. Oh, Talli had known for years that the sexy, gorgeous guy serving up the most delicious breakfast burritos in Albuquerque was way, way, way out of her league—especially when she'd seen him for the first time five years ago, when she'd been only fifteen and he'd probably already been twenty-five. She'd been jailbait then! Still, over the past couple of years, Talli had managed to lock eyes with the gorgeous hunk of breakfast burrito several times during the fiesta. He'd even smiled at her every day the year before! Therefore, she hoped he'd be working for Villarreal's again this year, if for no other reason than he was eye candy—the supreme kind of eye candy that got a girl through a day of making and serving funnel cake for eight to ten hours consecutively.

Another whiff of green chile filled her lungs, and Talli hurried down the incline pavement path toward the field. Another hour and the burritos oughta be ready. She figured Mike would have the hot water and hot chocolate mix all ready to serve when she got to the funnel cake stand. A cup or two of hot chocolate should hold her over until Villarreal's was ready to serve breakfast burritos. Still, as the scent of warm tortillas, green chile, scrambled eggs, sausage, and cheese became stronger and stronger, Talli began to hope that maybe the oil and funnel cake batter were already prepared—'cause her stomach was growling like a lumberjack's!

All at once, Talli felt the ball of her right foot catch on the pavement. As she stumbled forward, she tried to steady her footing, but it was too late. The downward slope of the paved path down to the field was just too steep, and she squealed a bit as she felt herself fall forward. As her stomach and chest collided with the ground, she felt her chin graze the pavement—felt her legs whip up over her back for a moment before she came to rest sprawled out like a cartoon character who had just hit a brick wall.

"Hey! Are you all right?" a deep voice asked.

Still struggling to draw breath—the awful panic of having the air pushed so forcibly from her lungs threatening to shove her into hysterics—Talli nodded, gasping, "Yeah…yeah…I'm fine."

"I don't think you're fine," the deep voice doubted.

Then Talli felt strong hands assisting her to roll over onto her back, as several other passersby stopped, each asking, "Are you okay?"

Talli's heart plunged to the bottom of her stomach. For as she found herself staring up into the gorgeous face of the hot Villarreal's burrito guy, she choked, "Hey…you're the Villarreal burrito boy."

The handsome breakfast burrito maker smiled. "And you're the funnel cake girl, right?"

"Yeah," Talli managed.

"Are you sure you're okay?" the handsome man inquired.

Talli was momentarily dazed into silence as she stared into his deep green eyes— studied his perfect nose, dazzling smile, black hair, and flawlessly trimmed four- or five-day facial hair.

At last she managed to respond, "Yep. Nothing's hurt more than my pride."

The sexy burrito guy chuckled, helping her to stand. "Well, it looks to me like maybe your chin is more hurt than anything else…which is kind of amazing, being that I watched you just totally scorpion."

"My chin?" Talli asked, putting a hand to her chin. Vaguely she remembered bumping it on the pavement. But when she looked at her hand to see a good amount of blood there, she sighed, "Oh great."

The sexy burrito guy frowned, carefully took hold of her chin, and studied it for a moment. "I think it's just a bad scrape." Reaching around to his back, he pulled a fry apron out of his waistband, wadding it up and pressing it to her chin. "Here, just press this against it for a minute or two. And I promise that it's clean. Well, I washed it last year after the fiesta anyway. It's been in the closet, so it might be dusty…but that's all."

"Thanks," Talli said, pressing the apron to her chin.

"You sure you're all right?" the kettle corn lady asked. "That was quite a tumble you took."

"Yeah," Talli agreed, blushing as red as a summer geranium. "I tend to do everything embarrassingly big."

"So you're not really a contortionist?" the sexy burrito guy asked, smiling at her. "Because the way you scorpioned…I would've sworn you were."

"Nope. I'm just the funnel cake girl," Talli said, forcing a smile. She felt like an idiot! It was bad enough she'd face-planted—and then obviously scorpioned, to boot—right in front of the sexy burrito guy, but now she stood there pressing his apron to her chin like some kindergartener who'd just wiped out on the playground at recess!

"Well, after a fall like that, I'm sure you could use some breakfast," the sexy burrito guy said. "So when you're all set up at your place, come over and have a burrito on me, before this place starts bouncing, okay?"

Talli smiled, shaking her head. "Oh no. I'm fine, really," she said—though the thought did cross her mind that maybe it wouldn't be too awful a thing to sit on the sexy burrito guy's lap while eating a burrito.

"No, seriously," the hunk of gorgeousness insisted. "Just give me have half an hour or so, and I'll have one ready for you. What do you want? The works? Eggs, sausage, cheese? Green or red?"

Laughing a little, Talli gave in. After all, she'd be insane to turn down a breakfast burrito made to order by the sexiest burrito guy in the world.

"Okay, you've tempted me, and I'm caving in," she said. "The works—but no potatoes—and green chile, of course. And I'll pay for it. It's what I was going to have for breakfast anyway."

"It's on me," the sexy burrito guy said. "I mean, that was a wicked fierce scorpion! It would have broken my back. So at least let me treat you to breakfast, okay?"

Blushing, Talli bit her lip and nodded. "Okay."

"Great," the sexy burrito guy said, smiling once more. "Like I said, in thirty minutes or so I'll have it ready for you."

"Okay, but you really don't have—" Talli began.

"I know," the sexy burrito guy interrupted. Then offering his hand to her—his large, powerful-looking, well-callused right hand—he said, "I'm Ruger."

Taking his hand, Talli asked, "Like the gun?"

The sexy burrito guy chuckled. "Yeah…like the gun."

"I'm Talli. And it's nice to meet you."

"Nice to meet you, Talli the funnel cake girl," Ruger said. He released her hand, and Talli was overcome by a sudden sensation of disappointment. After all, she'd touched the sexy burrito guy—actually touched him! Even shaken his hand! Not to mention the fact that he'd rolled her over after her less-than-graceful fall and scorpion, helping her up too.

"So half an hour or so?" he reiterated.

"Yes. And thanks so much," Talli said as she watched him pick up her backpack, coat, and apron.

Ruger the sexy burrito guy flashed a stunning set of pearly whites, handed Talli's stuff to her, and said, "Okay. See you then. And I hope your chin is okay."

"I'm sure it is," Talli insisted.

As he walked away, down the pavement path toward the field, Talli could only stand and stare at him—watch the way his broad, broad, way broad shoulders sort of teeter-tottered as he walked—the way he rather swaggered, though not intentionally.

"Well, he certainly knows how to buy jeans to flatter his physique, hmmm?" the kettle corn lady mumbled as she started toward the balloon field again, hurrying a bit to catch up with her husband, who was already some distance ahead of her.

The kettle corn lady glanced back over her shoulder to Talli, winking with understanding.

"Really, Talli?" Talli asked herself as she started down toward the field once more. "That's how you meet the sexy burrito guy after five years? By falling flat on your face?"

Still, she smiled a little as she continued on her way. At least she'd impressed him with her wicked fierce scorpion. And the soreness already beginning in her back was proof of it. Nevertheless, Talli surmised there was one good thing that came out of her embarrassing face-plant: Ruger the sexy burrito guy probably wouldn't forget her too quickly. At least not until after she'd picked up her breakfast burrito.

As her stomach growled with the anticipation of a delicious breakfast, Talli hurried the rest of the way to Vendors' Row. Finally! After five years of trying to steal glimpses of the sexy burrito guy who worked Villarreal's burrito stand during the balloon fiesta, she'd finally gotten a good, long look at him, up close and personal! And he was every bit as gorgeous-sexy as she'd remembered.

CHAPTER TWO

"Good morning, Rosie," Talli said as she entered the funnel cake stand via the back door.

"Good morning," Rosie cheerfully greeted. When she looked up from the vat of batter she was mixing a moment later, however, her dark eyebrows pinched together in an arch of concern. "What happened to you?"

"Who, me?" Talli shrugged. "Oh, I just finally met that sexy burrito guy who works the Villarreal stand this morning, that's all…by face-planting on the pavement right in front of him!"

"Oh no!" Rosie exclaimed, giggling a little as her expression changed to complete sympathy. "How badly did you get hurt?" Rosie stopped mixing the batter and strode to Talli. "Let me see it," she demanded.

Talli removed the hot burrito guy's wadded apron from her chin, frowning as Rosie winced while inspecting it.

Clicking her tongue, Rosie admitted, "Eeee! It looks pretty bad. But at least it's only a scrape. It's not like something you need stitches for or anything. It just kind of looks—"

"Like I'm six years old and wiped out on my bike, right?" Talli suggested.

Rosie smiled, nodded, and agreed, "Yeah…exactly like that."

"How embarrassing," Talli sighed. "Has it stopped bleeding, at least?"

"Pretty much," Rosie confirmed. Shaking her head, she added, "But it's, like, on the whole part of your chin. Good thing you're not a supermodel, huh?"

"Good thing," Talli said, smiling. "It kind of hurts more than I thought it would. Like…more and more."

Rosie smiled with compassion and went back to stirring the batter in the vat. "Well, at least you'll have a story to tell all the customers when you're at the order counter this week."

"Good morning, chicas!" Mike greeted as he entered the funnel cake stand as well. "Are you ready to fry?"

"Hi, Mike," Rosie greeted.

"Morning, Mike," Talli said, turning to face him.

"Eeee, Talli!" Mike exclaimed in perfect New Mexican singsong. "What happened?"

Talli couldn't help but smile. She loved the singsong intonation pattern of speech so prevalent in New Mexicans, especially native Albuquerqueians (including herself)—the way every exclamation, as well as the last few words of each sentence were stretched out with emphasis, accent, and inflection so that the speaker was kind of singing. Hundreds of years before, New Mexican Spanish and English merged together into what some linguist somewhere had recently dubbed Burqueño—the language of Burqueños-slash-Albuquerqueians. Talli figured that Burqueño was easier for most people to spell than Albuquerqueian. But whatever outsiders wanted to call it, Talli loved the New Mexican singsong as much as she loved her hometown, Albuquerque, and the state of New Mexico as a whole.

"I wiped out coming down the hill," Talli explained.

"Do you need stitches or no?" Mike asked, frowning with sincere concern.

"No, it's just a scrape," Talli explained.

"Are you sure?" Mike asked, still frowning.

Talli smiled. "I'm sure, Mike. But you're so cute to be concerned."

Rosie and Mike had been Talli's friends since middle school. And when they'd hit high school and Mike's dad had started selling funnel cakes at the fiesta as a one-week side business, Mike had headhunted Rosie and Talli to work the funnel cake stand with him. It had started as a great way to make extra money for the teenagers, as well as a way to be around the balloons as much as possible. Of course, now there were more workers, more shifts, and more money rolling in for Mike's dad, Mr. Gutierrez. But Rosie, Talli, and Mike still worked the stand every year. However, though it was unspoken for the most part, they now worked it for the balloons and camaraderie instead of extra money. The fact was, each of them had to exhaust a week's worth of vacation time from their regular jobs to do it. But to Talli, it was well worth the sacrifice. And she figured that Rosie and Mike felt the same way, or else they wouldn't continue to do it either.

"Well, maybe you should work the kitchen today so that you don't scare the customers away, huh?" Mike teased. " 'Cause Halloween ain't 'til the end of the month, you know."

"Ha ha. Very funny, Mike," Rosie said.

"I thought so," Mike said, grinning with being pleased with himself.

"Hey, at least you met the sexy burrito guy, right?" Rosie offered.

"Yeah. At least there's that," Talli agreed.

"Did he ask you out or what?" Mike asked.

"No, Mike. He didn't ask me out," Talli answered. "But he did lend me his apron to bleed all over."

"Well, there you go, chica! That proves that he's way into you," Mike said, patting Talli on the back.

"Oh, is that what that means?" Talli giggled. "I was hoping it was the free breakfast burrito I'm supposed to pick up in thirty minutes that means he might have noticed me. Although I don't know how he could've not noticed me. The way I scorpioned when I fell would've definitely made FailArmy on YouTube if someone had been filming."

"Oh man! You scorpioned?" Mike asked, wincing.

"Yep," Talli admitted. "But let's quit talking about what a doof I am. We've got funnel cake to make, right?"

"Yeah," Rosie agreed. "I've got the oil heating, Mike, and this is the first batch of batter. As soon as I get it in the fridge I'll start another one."

"Good," Mike said, looking around the interior of the stand. "Talli, why don't you fill the powdered sugar sifters? I'll bring in the rest of the plates and napkins. Looks like Dad has got the Coke fridge full already. So we should be good to go."

"I just hope the balloons fly," Talli said. "I always feel sick when they don't. People come so far, and then to be disappointed like that? It totally makes me feel so bad."

"They'll fly," Mike said assuredly. "The wind was only seven miles per hour when I checked just now on my way in. They'll fly."

Talli smiled at Mike. Poor guy! She knew that he felt as disappointed as the out-of-town visitors did when the wind was over eight miles per hour, meaning the balloons couldn't launch. Oh, he played the tough guy—and he looked it too, with all his weight-lifting muscles, black mustache and goatee, and dark black hair. Mike was a handsome man, but he was as tenderhearted about the balloon fiesta as Rosie and Talli were—no matter how hard he tried to appear otherwise.

"Hey," Mike said, reaching around to his back jeans pocket and retrieving his wallet. "When you go pick up your sympathy burrito, will you grab one with everything for me? Do you want one, Rosie? I'm buying."

"You bet!" Rosie exclaimed.

Mike handed Talli a twenty, asking, "Do you mind?"

"Of course not," Talli assured him. "That way I won't feel as bad about getting one for free, you know?"

"Oh, don't feel bad," Mike said. "You obviously earned it, right?"

Talli smiled, feeling a bit better about looking like a fool in front of Ruger the sexy burrito guy. "I suppose I did. And I can already tell you that I'm going to have the bruises and sore muscles to prove it."

"I've got the water heated already, if you guys want hot chocolate," Rosie offered as she shoved the giant vat of funnel cake batter into the industrial-sized refrigerator.

All at once, a little breeze wafted through the funnel cake stand. Instantly Rosie, Mike, and Talli stood very still, frowning at one another with concern.

"It'll die down," Mike said, trying to convince himself as well as Rosie and Talli that it would. "It'll die down. It's the first day of fiesta. It has to die down."

"It will die down," Rosie said, nodding and looking from Talli to Mike and back.

"Oh yeah. It will totally die down," Talli said, also nodding.

It was the one thing she didn't like about the balloon fiesta, the ever-lingering possibility that the beautiful Albuquerque weather wouldn't cooperate with the balloonists—that the wind would kick up and leave everyone in the city waiting on the edge of their seats to see whether it would be a glorious day of hundreds of balloons aloft or a why-did-we-get-up-this-early day as the balloonists gathered up their equipment and drove off the balloon field to everyone's bitter disappointment.

Still, in her heart, Talli felt all would be well that morning. The dark, starry sky was clear and beautiful, and the slight breeze was a steady seven miles per hour. They would fly; the balloons would fly that marvelous first Saturday in October. Talli knew they would.

♥

It wasn't far from the funnel cake stand to Villarreal's. In fact, it was only about twenty feet, being that the only thing between the two vendors was the paved path leading down from the parking lots. But as Talli crossed the short expanse of pavement, it felt like there were an ocean to cross because the sexy burrito guy, Ruger, was watching her—smiling at her—the entire time as she approached!

"Hui!" Talli exclaimed under her breath. "Could you be any more good-looking, sexy burrito guy? And must you stare at me the entire time I'm walking over to see you?" she quietly muttered.

But when the sexy burrito guy smiled at her, looking like he'd heard exactly what she'd been mumbling to herself, Talli felt herself blush. "Oh, I'm sure blushing does everything to accentuate my scraped-up chin too," she whispered.

Holy smokes, he was hot! That black hair of his, that square chin and jaw line, a smile that looked like it was made of fake dental veneers—he was gorgeous! Talli felt her stomach do a couple of flips as butterflies seemed to launch to flight in it. Sexy burrito guy's gorgeous green eyes were boring right through her, and Talli was afraid she'd biff it again if she weren't careful. How embarrassing would that be, she thought. Therefore she made sure she walked casually yet cautiously—if such a thing were even possible—because Talli was determined not to dork out again in front of the guy she'd been admiring from afar for five years.

Ruger couldn't help but smile as he watched the cute funnel cake girl walk toward him. She was way too attractive for her own good, especially with her soft brown hair pulled up into a ponytail. He felt his smile broaden, amused by the way her ponytail swung back and forth in rhythm with her walking. She was wearing the same black sweatshirt she wore every morning of the balloon fiesta—for the past five years—a faded, ratty-looking black sweatshirt with Dracula Sucks! printed on the front.

Ruger's internal delight increased as he looked forward to watching her strip throughout the day. Everyone who worked the fiesta would do it; it was necessary, especially if a body worked in one of the vendor stands. It was pretty chilly at four a.m. in October in Albuquerque. Therefore, for his part, Ruger always arrived at the burrito stand wearing a sweatshirt as well. But by the time the kitchen was heated up and the balloons were aloft, he was nearly sweltering and therefore would strip his sweatshirt off, revealing the T-shirt he wore beneath.

But there were a lot more layers to the hot little chica from the funnel cake stand. Every year for the past five years, he'd enjoyed watching her begin working in some sort of sweatshirt. By the time the sun was beginning to rise over the Sandia Mountains to the east, she'd have stripped off her sweatshirt to reveal a red long-sleeved Nebraska Cornhuskers T-shirt beneath. By the time the balloons were aloft, she'd have stripped off the long-sleeved T-shirt and would be wearing a plain white T-shirt. By noon when her regular shift always seemed to be over, the white t-shirt would've had the sleeves rolled up and the long, excess fabric of the torso tied into a knot at her waist. It was a routine Ruger had grown to really enjoy.

And now—now that she was smiling and walking toward him to collect her complementary breakfast burrito—he chuckled quietly, excited about the predictability of working at the fiesta. Everybody dressed in layers, even visitors from out of town. But for some reason, the emergence of the funnel cake girl from her layered cocoon always entertained him most.

"How you doing?" Ruger asked as the pretty little thing named Talli reached the north side of the stand.

"I'm well," Talli said, smiling at him. "A little scraped up, but fine."

She held out the apron Ruger had given to her to help her chin stop bleeding, saying, "Do you want this back? I mean, it's all nasty now with my blood all over it. I could take it home and wash it for you and bring it back tomorrow."

"Naw. That's okay," Ruger said, accepting the apron and tossing it into the bin meant for dirty aprons at the back of the stand. "A little blood doesn't bother me."

"Well, don't clone me, okay?" Talli nervously giggled.

As the sexy burrito guy laughed, Talli silently scolded herself for uttering such a stupid joke. Still, he seemed amused, so she simply tried to regain her composure.

"Oh!" she exclaimed, remembering Mike's money. "I need two burritos with everything for my friends, if you guys have any ready yet."

Ruger smiled at her, reached beneath the counter, and handed her one fat, cylindrically foil-wrapped breakfast burrito.

"Here's yours first," he said. He turned, calling over his shoulder, "Colt! You got two everythings ready yet?"

"Almost," a man's voice called from the far side of the stand.

"It'll be just a minute," Ruger said.

"Colt?" Talli asked. "What? Is he your brother or something? I mean…Ruger and Colt? It can't be a coincidence, right?"

Ruger nodded. "Yep. He's my brother. My parents are diehard gun enthusiasts," he said.

"Oh wow! I guess so," Talli stammered, feeling ridiculous. She hoped he didn't think she'd been making fun of their names.

"Ruger Villarreal," Ruger said, offering his hand to her.

"Villarreal?" Talli said as she took his hand. "Like…in this breakfast burrito stand, Villarreal?"

"Yeah," Ruger said, still holding her hand. "It's my brother's place. He started it five years ago. He only does it at the fiesta…but he makes bank, you know?"

"I do know," Talli confirmed. "Mr. Gutierrez, the man who owns the funnel cake stand I work at, only does the fiesta too. But, as you know, it's well worth it financially." Realizing that Ruger still hadn't let go of her hand, she added, "Oh! And I'm Talli Chaucer, by the way."

Still holding her hand, but shaking it a little this time, Ruger said, "Well, it's nice to meet you, Talli Chaucer. How's your chin feeling?"

"Fine. Just kind of stiff," Talli admitted as Ruger released her hand.

"I'll bet," Ruger said.

"Here you go," a man looking a lot like Ruger said as he stepped up behind him. "Hi. I'm Colt," he said with a nod to Talli as he laid two more foil-wrapped burritos on the counter.

"I'm Talli," she said in return.

"Those are hot, so be careful, okay?" Colt Villarreal warned with a friendly smile.

"Thank you," Talli told him. "And can I just tell you that you guys have the best breakfast burritos I've ever tasted? They are so good! I swear I eat a dozen every year during the fiesta."

"Wow, thanks! I'm glad you like them," Colt said, his smile broadening. "And those are on the house, by the way," he added.

"Oh no, no, no," Talli said, digging the twenty out of the front pocket of her jeans. "I've got it. You can't make any money if you keep giving away your product, you know."

"How about you take these for now and owe me a couple of funnel cakes later, huh?" Colt suggested.

"Are you sure?" Talli asked.

"Absolutely," Colt said.

"Well, all right. But if you don't show up to get them by noon, I'll bring them over before I leave...after my shift, okay?"

"Sounds good," Colt agreed. "See you later."

"You too," Talli called as Colt turned and hurried toward the other side of the stand.

"Well, here you go," Ruger said, picking up the three burritos and offering them to Talli.

Cramming Mike's twenty back into her pocket, Talli said, "Thanks," as she accepted the food. "Here's hoping you have a busy morning," Talli giggled as she turned to leave.

"Hey, Talli," Ruger called, stalling her, however.

"Yeah?" Talli turned back around to face the sexy burrito guy, and the sight of him caused her arms to break out in goose bumps.

"Um...you say your shift ends at noon?" he asked.

"Yeah," she affirmed.

"Well, I figure, if you're like me, you'll be worn out and need a nap," he began, "but would you let me take you out to eat for dinner tonight? Like maybe around six or so?"

"Are you serious?" Talli asked, wondering if she were imagining the conversation.

Ruger laughed. "Yeah, I'm serious. I figure…we've been scoping each other out for five years or better…and you've gotta be beyond jailbait age by now, right?"

"Right," Talli giggled. "Several years beyond it, actually."

"Good. Then how about dinner? It can be simple…maybe Dion's?" he suggested.

"I love Dion's!" Talli exclaimed. "Yeah, that would be awesome. Should I meet you somewhere?"

"How about you stop by when you finish your shift and we'll work out the details, okay?" Ruger asked.

"Okay," Talli agreed. Holding up the three burritos she held, she said, "And thanks again, Ruger."

"Oh, you're quite welcome, Talli," he said.

"Bye," Talli said, blushing a little as he winked at her, giving her the traditional Albuquerque chin-thrust gesture of see-you-later in response.

As Talli headed back toward the funnel cake stand, she felt more like she were walking on air than pavement. The sexy burrito guy had just asked her out! Five years of mooning after a complete stranger—spending a whole week every year dreaming that one day he'd notice her and ask her out—had come to glorious fruition! And all because Talli had been a dork and unintentionally performed a painful, and obviously wicked fierce, scorpion there on the pavement the first morning of the balloon fiesta!

CHAPTER THREE

"He asked you out to dinner…at Dion's?" Rosie squeaked as Talli handed her a Villarreal's breakfast burrito. "Eee, girl! After all these years, you've finally spoken to him…and now he's taking you to dinner? Wow!"

"I know, huh?" Talli said, handing Mike his burrito. "I still can't believe it."

"I guess it was worth humiliating yourself in front of him this morning, huh," Mike chuckled as he tore into the foil at one end of his burrito. Hardly taking a breath between peeling back the foil and taking a monster bite, Mike moaned, "Mmmmm! I don't know why those Villarreal guys don't open a restaurant. Their burritos are easily the best in the city."

Talli's mouth began to water with anticipation as she peeled open the foil at one end of her burrito. Deeply inhaling the aroma of the burrito first—to ensure full enjoyment of what she was about to eat—she smiled and sighed, "They really are! And they don't scrimp on the green chile either."

Taking her first bite of the mouthwatering, savory breakfast burrito, Talli sighed again as the perfectly paired flavors of a handmade flour tortilla, scrambled eggs, fried sausage, onion, green pepper, cheddar cheese, and the magnificent, distinctive zest of green chile blended together in her mouth, causing goose bumps to prickle her scalp. It was that delicious—goose-bumpingly delicious!

"Man! These are always so good!" she exclaimed. "Why is it breakfast burritos never taste as good the rest of the year? Only Villarreal's at the balloon fiesta taste like this, you know?"

"Kind of like how hot dogs really only taste good at UNM football games, right?" Rosie offered.

There were long moments of consecutive silence then as Talli, Mike, and Rosie savored the familiar, glorious flavor of Villarreal's balloon fiesta breakfast burritos. Talli wondered how on earth the green chile breakfast burrito hadn't taken over the entire country! As much as she loved pancakes and bacon, they always left her feeling tired and still hungry. Yet a good breakfast burrito had content, protein, staying power, and a whole lot more flavor. Still, she knew that most people had some sort of food thing from their hometown or state that they loved far more than any visitor ever did. But a balloon fiesta breakfast burrito—even from the vendors other than the Villarreal's—Talli just couldn't understand why the whole world wasn't jumping on the bandwagon.

"It's like a total experience, you know?" Rosie said as she chewed. "Mmmm!"

"I should've had you get me two, Talli," Mike mumbled with his mouth full.

Just then a lady with a thick French accent approached the ordering window of the funnel cake stand, asking, "When do you start serving this morning?"

Talli swallowed her burrito bite quickly and answered, "Five a.m., ma'am. About another fifteen minutes, okay?"

"Thank you," the French lady said with a smile.

"See, Mike? You won't have time to down another one," Rosie said.

"I know, but still…mmmm!" Mike again moaned with a full mouth.

Quickly, and in silence (with the exception of an occasional "Mmmm!" emanating from one of their throats), Talli, Rosie, and Mike hurriedly finished their burritos. They needed to be ready to fry and serve by five, and the clock was ticking. In an hour the dawn patrol would launch, and the pre-dawn patrol crowd was always voracious for breakfast—even for funnel cake.

Talli wiped her mouth with a paper napkin, tossed her burrito foil in the nearby garbage can, and headed toward the stove to check the temperature of the oil in the four skillets. Dipping a little of Rosie's newest batter out of the vat with a small spoon, Talli drizzled a little into each skillet, smiling as the sound of frying funnel cake batter sizzled into the cool morning air.

"Oil looks good to go," she called.

"Awesome!" Mike said. He glanced around the interior of the stand, nodding and saying, "I think everything's in order. I've got the till all set up—plenty of change and ones, I hope—so we should be good to go."

"Oh! That reminds me," Talli said, hurrying back to Mike as she retrieved his twenty-dollar bill from her front pocket. "Here. Ruger didn't charge me for our burritos, but he'll be by later for some funnel cakes. Okay?"

"Ruger?" Mike and Rosie chimed in unison.

"His name is Ruger?" Mike asked. "Like the gun guy?"

"Yep," Talli giggled. "Ruger Villarreal."

"Villarreal?" Mike and Rosie chimed in unison again.

"Like in the Villarreals who own the breakfast burrito stand?" Rosie asked.

"Yep. His brother owns it," Talli explained.

Mike chuckled. "And what's his brother's name? Winchester?" Mike nudged Rosie with one elbow, whispering, "Winchester. Get it?"

"I get it, you idiot," Rosie said, smiling and rolling her eyes.

"Actually, his brother's name is Colt," Talli explained.

"Colt?" Mike and Rosie again chimed in perfect synchronicity.

Talli couldn't help but laugh. It had been the same since the three of them had been juniors in high school. That was the year that Mike and Rosie became true soul mates, and Talli wondered if and when the two of them would ever figure out what everybody else already knew—that they were made for each other!

"It's true. His name is Colt. I even met him," Talli said.

"One painful scorpion, three free burritos, an invitation to dinner, and you're already meeting his family?" Rosie squealed. "How romantic!"

Now it was Talli who rolled her eyes and laughed. "Oh yeah, that's it, Rosie—romantic. That's exactly the word for it. Especially when I look like I just rolled out of bed and found my clothes shoved in between the cushions of the couch. Yeah, romantic. I'm sure that's what sexy burrito man has in mind for me…romance."

Mike and Rosie exchanged glances, and Mike shrugged. "Well, I wouldn't ask a girl to Dion's for dinner unless I was serious about getting to know her better."

"Dion's?" Rosie exclaimed. "That's your idea of a serious get-to-know-you dinner?"

Mike looked perplexed as he stared at Rosie. "I love Dion's. Don't you?"

"Yeah, but...I don't know. Maybe if you asked me to the Melting Pot or something, then I would think you were serious about getting to know me," Rosie said.

Mike frowned. "But I already know you."

Talli giggled. Watching Mike and Rosie together was like watching a sitcom half of the time.

"Well, I love Dion's too," Talli said. "And I would've been flattered if he'd offered to take me to the churros stand three vendors down from us. I mean, I never in a million years thought I'd ever find myself face to face with him, let alone talking to him."

"Let alone falling flat on your face in front of him," Mike added with a smile.

"Shut up, Mike," Rosie said, jabbing an elbow into Mike's ribcage.

But Talli shrugged. "Hey, if all it takes is some major humiliation and looking like someone went at my chin with a cheese grater to find me in the company of Ruger Villarreal at Dion's tonight...I'm down with that."

Rosie smiled. "Well, you don't look like someone took a cheese grater to your chin," Rosie said as she returned to mixing a vat of funnel cake batter.

"You really don't," Mike agreed. "You look like you were hauling it down a hill on your trike and wiped out."

Mike winked at her teasingly, and Talli laughed. After all, she figured things could've been worse. She could've scorpioned, face-planted on the pathway, and had Ruger Villarreal roll her over to find the pavement had shaved her nose off.

♥

As "The Star-Spangled Banner" began to play over the sound system, announcing the launch of the dawn patrol, Talli, Mike, and

Rosie stood with their hands over their hearts. Some people were singing along to the national anthem, others simply standing in awe as the first balloon of the dawn patrol began to slowly rise into the still-dark sky. Once the first balloon had launched, unfurling the American flag from one side of the balloon basket—once the national anthem had ended and everyone still on the ground began to cheer as the balloon's pilot laid on the burner, the fire from it lighting up the inside of the hot air balloon as it heated the air inside—Talli and her friends joined the applause. One by one the other members of the dawn patrol launched, and soon the balloons whose pilots would keep tabs on the weather and look for ideal landing areas lazily drifted overhead, looking like giant light bulbs blinking on and off with the beautiful orange glow as the burners' sporadic puffs of fire lit them.

Talli knew she was grinning like an idiot, but she didn't care. The launch of the dawn patrol was the indicator the pilots were "good to launch." The weather was perfect! And any moment the sun would breach the crest of the Sandia Mountains to the east, and then—then the throng of hot air balloons would begin to inflate, lingering on the seventy-eight-acre launch field until they were given the go for launch. What would follow was something to behold indeed, and Talli never tired of watching the six-hundred-plus hot air balloons of varying size, shapes, and colors lift into the air to begin drifting over the city of Albuquerque.

"I need five!" Rosie called from the order counter.

"I'm on it!" Mike hollered as he began drizzling batter into four of the skillets filled with hot oil.

Mike's cousins Lorraine and Josh entered the stand by way of the back door then.

"Órale, Mike," Josh greeted.

"Órale, vato," Mike greeted in return. "Did you guys get stuck in traffic or what?"

"Oh, you know it, bro," Josh said, removing his jacket and hanging it on a hook by the stand's back door. He smiled at Talli then. "Hey, Talli. How's it going?"

"Busy!" Talli greeted in response.

"Hi, Talli," Lorraine said, giving Talli a quick hug. "It's so good to see you."

"You too, Lorraine," Talli sincerely replied.

"Where should we start, man?" Josh asked Mike.

"Why don't you help me fry?" Mike said. "Talli, you wanna work the counter with Rosie a bit and Lorraine can put on the powdered sugar and serve?"

"You bet," Talli agreed.

As she paused at the sink to wash her hands, Talli looked up and toward the Villarreal stand across the pavement path.

As fate would have it, Ruger was serving up orders and happened to glance up just as Talli looked his way. As a handsome, dazzling smile spread across his face, Talli smiled in return, giggling when he tossed a chin-thrust in greeting to her. She offered the same gesture back, and he winked before returning his attention to the customer he was serving. He was so stinking handsome! It wasn't fair to all the other men on earth, Talli thought—to have to compete with such a tall, dark, and handsome piece of beefcake like Ruger Villarreal.

Drying her hands, Talli hurried to the order counter. She knew there would be a huge rush for half an hour to forty-five minutes while the pilots were laying out their balloons' envelopes on the field, prepping to fill them with hot air and then launch when they were given the green light to do so. But forty-five minutes of hard work was well worth it to be so close to the field, to hear the burners heating the air, to see the expressions of pure joy and amazement on the faces of the thousands of people gathered to watch and photograph the event when the balloons did begin the mass ascension. It was well worth being tired and overheated, wrung out by the end of the week, and let down when it was all over. It was a once-in-a-lifetime sort of thing for most people and the thing Talli looked forward to every year more than anything else—even, perhaps, Christmas!

"I heard you finally met up with the sexy burrito guy from Villarreal's," Lorraine said as Talli headed toward the order counter.

Talli laughed. "How did you already hear that?"

"Rosie texted me, of course," Lorraine said, smiling. "Good job, girl! He is so hot! I can't believe he's not already taken, you know?"

"I know, huh?" Talli admitted.

"I guess he's just been waiting for the right funnel cake girl or what?" Lorraine giggled. "Right?"

"I hope so," Talli laughed.

Then facing the crowd that had gathered in front of the order counter in only a matter of moments since Talli had arrived, she asked, "Can I help who's next, please?"

By seven a.m. and the start of the first mass ascension of the year, Talli was wondering how she was ever going to make it through the next five hours! Sure, the lines waiting to order funnel cake would die down to just a drizzle for a while, but once all the balloons had launched, people would really be ready to munch! Yet as Talli plopped down in a plastic chair to slam down a bottled water, she glanced over to see that the Villarreal's stand was still pumping—even for the fact that the balloons were beginning to launch in the usual waves.

"Híjole! I'm glad we don't work over there, no?" Mike said, collapsing into the chair next to Talli. "Those guys never get a break."

"I know, huh?" Talli agreed as she watched Ruger passing out burritos and taking more orders at the speed of light. "I'll stick with funnel cake."

"Me too," Mike agreed. "I'm so tired! I hope it stays died down for a while, you know?"

"I do," Talli said.

As she sat relaxing for the few minutes allotted her, Talli drank the cold water from her water bottle and watched Ruger work. Talli had taken off her sweatshirt already but was still cool enough to keep the long-sleeved T-shirt she was wearing on over her regular T-shirt. Ruger Villarreal, however, had traded his sweatshirt in for just a T-shirt an hour before—and Talli was glad. She liked watching the muscles in his forearms and the part of his biceps she could see peeking out from under his T-shirt sleeve ripple and move as he worked. He was very broad-shouldered, and she wondered then what he did for a living. Was he a personal trainer, perhaps? He sure looked the part—toned to the bone like stone and as good-looking as hell! But he didn't seem the type—didn't seem to have the ego. Maybe somebody else would think Talli didn't have any way of knowing what Ruger Villarreal's ego was or wasn't like, but she did. Talli had studied the man for five years, and never had she seen him be anything but polite and patient with customers. He always seemed to pamper the elderly people at the balloon fiesta, and in Talli's experience, egotistical jerks didn't treat elderly people with any respect, let alone pamper them with extra napkins or helping them to find a place to sit while they ate.

Nope. Ruger wasn't the prideful, conceited type. And by the way he ate breakfast burritos and funnel cake, she figured he wasn't a personal trainer, simply for the fact that he didn't seem to worry about good nutrition—at least not during the fiesta.

The crowd on the field began to cheer, and Talli looked away from Ruger and toward the place in the center of the field where the three Little Bees were inflated and ready to launch. The Little Bees were some of Talli's favorite special shapes balloons. It seemed most of the fiesta attendees favored the three brightly colored, smiling bees. The bees were not only enormous but often launched together, even while holding hands. Of course, Talli loved them most because the pilots frequently maneuvered the two largest bee balloons into kissing while floating above the balloon field. It was a real crowd-pleasing stunt, and Talli understood why.

"Can I run out real quick while the bees launch, Mike?" Talli asked. After all, working the funnel cake stand wouldn't be worth it if there weren't moments of hot air balloon enjoyment along with it.

"Yes, yes, yes," Mike said. "Don't you disappear every year when the bees launch?"

Talli smiled and said, "Thanks," snatching a ratty-looking funnel cake that hadn't turned out pretty enough to sell and had been sitting on the plate for the employees to pick at while they worked.

"Hey!" Mike teased as Talli hurried out of the stand and toward the field.

It was much colder on the balloon field than it had been in the funnel cake stand, but Talli didn't care. The cool, refreshing air of October in Albuquerque was invigorating, and she savored it. October and the balloon fiesta were both too fleeting for Talli's liking, and each year she relished both to whatever extreme she could.

"Hey, wait up," a newly familiar voice called from behind her.

Talli turned to see Ruger striding toward her, still wearing his white cook's apron.

"You like the bees, huh?" he asked.

"I love them!" Talli admitted.

"Me too. Do you mind if I come along?" Ruger asked.

"Not at all," Talli answered, her insides beginning to tremble—not from the cold but from the fact that the guy she'd google-eyed over for five years was walking with her out onto the balloon field.

"It's cold, but it's still good if you want some," she said, offering the flimsy paper plate with the cold funnel cake on it to him.

"Yeah, thanks," he said. He didn't take the plate from her but helped her support it as he tore off a piece of funnel cake. "Mmm! I love this stuff. I gain weight every year because of it."

"Me too!" Talli giggled. "Though your burritos are what really pack the extra tonnage on me. But they're so good, I can't resist!"

"That's how I feel about your funnel cakes," Ruger said.

"Oh, I'm glad," Talli giggled. "Funnel cake is all about joy, you know what I mean?"

"I do," Ruger chuckled.

The pilots of the Little Bees balloons fired their burners, and the balloons' envelopes began to rise from the field to stand erect over the burners and baskets, causing everyone to cheer.

"Here they go," Talli said with excitement.

"You don't photograph it at all or what?" Ruger asked, smiling as he tore another piece of funnel cake from the plate.

"Of course I do!" Talli assured him. "Do you?"

"Of course I do!" Ruger playfully mocked. "I work the first mass ascension of the fiesta every year and take the second one off in the morning and work the afternoon instead."

"So...you're off tomorrow?" Talli asked.

"Yeah. You?" he inquired in return.

"I am," Talli answered. "I usually take the second weekend mornings off to just be here and take pictures. But remember last year..."

"Ooo, bad news, huh? The balloons didn't fly either day the last two days last year," he said, shaking his head. "I bet you were bummed."

"I was," Talli admitted. "That's why I'm not taking any chances this year and took tomorrow morning off—actually, all day tomorrow off."

"Smart move," Ruger said. "Hey, you know what I was thinking? Our shifts today both end at noon, right?"

"Yeah?" Talli asked, her heart beginning to hammer inside her chest. What had he been thinking? Would he move their Dion's dinner date up to a lunch date? Talli was somewhat disappointed at the fact, simply because she usually looked like a half-rotted rat by the end of her shift. Still, she wasn't about to say no if that was what Ruger intended to suggest.

"Well, why don't you let me treat you to lunch here? We can have Frito pie or something, and then still let me take you out to Dion's for dinner," he suggested. "That way we can both enjoy some sunshine and fresh air after being trapped in vendors' stands all morning and then do dinner later. Or is that too much for you? I don't want you to think I'm a stalker or something."

Talli bit her lip to keep from squealing with delight! He was asking her on two dates in one day? Well, one date and a Frito pie lunch in one day, anyway. The stars must've perfectly aligned the night before, just for her sake.

"That would be great!" she told him. "Are you sure? I mean, you'll be tired after working all morning and—"

"Oh, believe me, I'm sure," Ruger said. He winked at her, tore another piece of funnel cake from what remained on the paper plate, and popped it in his mouth.

Talli blushed and was glad that the cheers of the crowd as the Little Bees rose slowly into the air distracted Ruger long enough for her to regain her composure.

"And there they go," he said as the Little Bees rose more quickly. "Whoo hooo!" he shouted, clapping his hands with everyone else nearby. "It never gets old, you know?"

"I know, huh?" Talli said. Her smile was so broad she thought her face might snap in two! She was standing there next to the sexy burrito guy she'd spent so many years daydreaming over, and she had two dates with him—two!

All at once, a whiff of green chile washed over her, and she inadvertently sighed, "Mmmm!"

"What's that?" Ruger asked.

"I just got a whiff of green chile," Talli explained. "I love that smell!"

"Well, then you oughta love me then," Ruger said.

Talli's eyes widened as Ruger held his powerful-looking hands up near her face.

"See? I was chopping chile before I took my break," he explained.

Talli sniffed his hands. Sure enough, the wonderful aroma of green chile was emanating from Ruger!

"How perfect is that?" Talli asked with a giggle.

"I have a bunch of chiles in sandwich baggies for people who want extra," he explained. "Come with me on our way back, and I'll give you one. If you want one, that is. I mean, some people don't eat it plain like I do, but—"

"I love it just by itself and on almost everything, so I would love a bag!" Talli gushed as her mouth began to water at the very thought of some green chile to munch on.

Ruger felt his smile broaden. He liked this girl! Already she loved three of his own favorite things: the balloon fiesta, funnel cake, and green chile. And she looked so adorable with powdered sugar all over her arms and face—even in her hair—smiling up at the Little Bees balloons and obviously sincere in her adoration of them.

Ruger had had a feeling simmering in his gut ever since he'd rolled her over after she'd biffed it on the pavement that morning. It was almost as if… He was afraid to even think it because it seemed so implausible, so impossible. But in that moment, something had whispered to him that this girl was the one—theee one—and he better strike while the iron was hot, then and there, that day, that morning. And so he had. Furthermore, Ruger figured if the hot little chica whom he'd been eyeing up for the past five years would agree to go out with him not once but twice in one day, then maybe she was having the same kind of premonitions he was having.

He studied Talli Chaucer as she stuffed a big piece of funnel cake into her mouth as she watched the Little Bees rise higher and higher into the beautiful blue of Albuquerque's morning October sky. Her eyes were the same brown as chocolate—he would swear to it—and she was overall just the cutest, prettiest, freshest girl he'd ever seen.

The cheer of the crowd rose, and Ruger looked up to see the two largest Little Bees kissing—and he was simply overwhelmed with another powerful moment of intuition. Looking back to Talli Chaucer, again something whispered to him that this was the girl meant for him—that after five years of watching and studying her, admiring her from afar, the time had come when they were both ready for what was meant to be between them.

As goose bumps broke over Ruger's arms, he was, in truth, a little unsettled. He'd arrived at Colt's breakfast burrito stand that morning hoping that the cute girl who worked the funnel cake stand would be there for the sixth year in a row—and now he was envisioning her dressed in a white wedding gown and doing the wedding march thing toward him? It was crazy! Yet it was what he was thinking—what he was feeling.

As more and more balloons began to launch around them, Ruger thought that life was like that most of the time. Just when you thought nothing extraordinary was ever going to happen—boom! The cute funnel cake girl biffed it right in front of you and you were handed the opportunity to meet her—to meet her—the one.

CHAPTER FOUR

Once all the hot air balloons had launched via the mass ascension, funnel cake sales slowed down a bit. While the majority of Albuquerque natives left soon after the mass ascension—heading home for a long nap after such an exciting morning—out-of-state visitors lingered in eating, purchasing collectable souvenirs, and enjoying live music and other events that were planned to make the trip well worth the time and money. Thus, those who worked in Mr. Gutierrez's funnel cake stand were allowed more frequent as well as longer breaks once all the balloons were aloft.

Being that Talli had already taken her first break to watch the launching of the Little Bees—and in the heavenly company of Ruger "The Sexy Burrito Guy" Villarreal—at eight thirty a.m. Rosie was on break. With just a few customers trickling here and there, Mike, Josh, Lorraine, and Talli relaxed a bit in the plastic lawn chairs inside the stand for a while.

"Eee, girl!" Lorraine exclaimed, shaking her head. "Two dates with him in one day? Are you lucky or what?"

Talli smiled. "Lucky and what, I guess."

"Oh, what's the big thing?" Mike asked. "It's not like he's the guy you're going to end up marrying, Talli."

"How do you know, Mike?" Lorraine asked defensively. "What if Talli does end up marrying him? Hmmm? It could happen."

Mike shrugged. "I suppose it could. Hey, Josh, throw me a Coke."

Talli watched, smiling as Josh leaned back in his chair, opened the beverages refrigerator, and removed an Orange Crush in a can.

"This one?" Josh asked Mike.

"No, man, the red Coke," Mike said.

Josh returned the Orange Crush to the refrigerator, retrieving a Strawberry Crush instead. He tossed it to Mike and then asked Lorraine, "Do you want a Coke?"

"Yeah," Lorraine said. "A brown one."

Josh reached into the refrigerator once more and retrieved a root beer. "Here you go," he said, tossing it to Lorraine. He looked to Talli next, asking, "Talli? You want something?"

"No. I've got my water, thanks," Talli said. As always she was amused by the way everyone in her hometown referred to every brand and flavor of soda pop as "a Coke."

Everyone startled when Rosie suddenly burst in through the back door.

"Talli!" she exclaimed, panting from the exertion of hurrying. "You have got to see this! You're not going to believe it! I mean, you have got to see this!"

"What?" Talli asked, rather disturbed. Jumping up from her chair, she asked again, "What?"

"What the hell, Rosie?" Mike growled. "You about gave me a heart attack!"

"Sorry, Mike," Rosie said aside to Mike. Then taking Talli by the shoulders and with eyes as wide as Frisbees, she said, "Talli...did you know?"

"Did I know what?" Talli asked, completely perplexed.

"Did you know that your sexy burrito guy is a professional chainsaw wood-carver?"

"What?" Talli laughed. "What are you talking about, Rosie?"

"You've got to come and see him! He's, like, awesome! He's doing it right now! He's out there with a chainsaw, going at a big old log thing, as part of the chainsaw carving invitational the fiesta holds every year. You have got to see this! They're all doing that thing where they have four minutes to carve something and then thirty minutes to carve something. He's on the thirty-minute thing right now! He already won the four-minute thing for this amazing raccoon he carved. You have to come see this!"

Talli stood entirely flabbergasted. Glancing over to the Villarreal's stand, she saw that indeed Ruger was not at his usual place shuffling out breakfast burritos.

Looking to Mike, she asked, "Can I go, Mike? I won't be gone long."

Mike smiled and rolled his eyes, saying, "Ahh! Young love. Of course you can go." Waving at her that she should leave, he added, "Go on. Go watch your new boyfriend hack at a log with a chainsaw. We're good here for a while."

"Thanks, Mike," Talli said, racing out through the stand's back door after Rosie.

"I couldn't believe it when I realized it was him, Talli!" Rosie exclaimed as the two young women hurried toward the carving area. "In fact, I wasn't sure until he won the four-minute contest and they announced his name. Then he took off his mouth and eye protection, and I about died right there! I mean, híjole, you know?"

For her part, Talli was still dazed. Ruger was a professional chainsaw wood-carver? Had he been entering the chainsaw carving invitational at the fiesta all the years that Talli had been gawking at him?

"Wow," Talli mumbled to herself as she and Rosie reached the carving venue. It was a noisy event. In fact, the reason Talli had never popped over to watch it all the years she worked the funnel cake stand was because of the noise. Oh, the sound of chainsaws in the distance wasn't a bad thing. But when they went for three or four hours every time Talli was working the funnel cake stand, it began to grate on her nerves. So she'd just never gone to watch the chainsaw wood-carvers do their thing.

But now as she stood there at the carving venue, her attention focused on the tall, dark, and handsome chainsaw carver nearest to where she and Rosie were standing—as she immediately recognized the muscular forearms and biceps working the chainsaw, recognized the uber-cool mannerisms and stance of Ruger Villarreal—her mouth literally dropped open in astonishment.

"I heard these guys can make a year's salary just from the auctions of their stuff here at the fiesta!" Rosie shouted over the roar of the chainsaws.

Yet Talli was still too awed to utter anything other than another, "Wow!"

As she stood with Rosie watching Ruger expertly sculpt what so far looked to be a tree with some sort of animals in it, Talli studied him from head to toe—from the hearing-protecting earmuffs he wore to his plastic eye goggles to the white carpenter's mask covering his mouth to the dark green chainsaw safety chaps covering his legs from the waist down. As if the man hadn't already won the "God's Gift to Women" award, he had a manly profession like chainsaw carver? Holy smokes! What smelled better on a man than the woodsy scent of wood, huh?

Ruger stopped carving for a moment, stepping back to inspect the project so far. And when he happened to look up inadvertently toward Talli, Talli smiled when he did a chin-thrust in her direction.

Hi, she mouthed, smiling.

He was back to work then, hacking away at an enormous vertically placed log with his chainsaw.

Goose bumps began to emerge over every inch of Talli's body, and a voice in her head whispered, This is the guy! This is the guy you've been waiting for!

Frowning, for she must've been losing her mind or, worse, slipping into schizophrenia—why else would she be hearing voices?—Talli tried to fight the growing affirmation inside her, affirmation that the sexy burrito guy was the one man who would make her happy in life. Sure, she'd stared at him for five years, but she'd only just met him that morning, mere hours before—only talked to him, what, three times? She absolutely had to be losing it! And yet the feeling lingered; she even felt a mounting sense of peace wash over her as she watched Ruger carve.

"What's wrong?" Rosie shouted. "Are you okay, Talli?"

Talli nodded, forced a smile, and shouted, "Yeah…just astonished, you know."

"I can imagine," Rosie answered.

Talli watched Ruger carve for a few more minutes. But when she looked back to see a line forming at the order counter of the funnel cake stand, she exhaled a heavy sigh and shouted to Rosie, "I better get back. Let me know how it turns out, okay?"

"I will," Rosie assured her.

Then, rather dismally, Talli turned and hurried back to help the others at the stand. But even as she jogged along Vendors' Row, she shook her head with disbelief. Could Ruger Villarreal get any more wonderful? And what was with her brain anyway? Thinking that Ruger was the one? Talli figured she just had first-morning-of-working-the-fiesta fatigue or something. That made a lot more sense than she'd all of a sudden developed psychic powers—which is exactly what the voice in her head felt like, some psychic phenomenon. Realistically, Talli knew she had just so, so, so wanted to get to know Ruger for so, so, so long that her brain was daydreaming without telling her. Either way, it had been a weird experience, and she knew she would spend the rest of her shift trying to shake it off somehow.

♥

However, thirty minutes later when Rosie returned to the funnel cake stand, announcing that Ruger Villarreal had also won the thirty-minute competition, Talli still hadn't been able to flush away the premonitory voice that was echoing, albeit much more quietly, in the back of her mind. At long last, near the end of her shift, Talli was just too tired to worry about it anymore. Maybe she really was meant to meet and be with Ruger, the sexy burrito guy. Of course, maybe she was just way tired from working the early shift on the first day of the fiesta. Still, whatever it was, by noon, Talli really was just too worn out to worry.

Therefore, when she stepped out through the back door of the funnel cake stand at noon—when she looked up to see Ruger leaning against the metal post behind the stand waiting for her—Talli simply smiled and decided to forget all the nonsense bopping around in her head and just have a good time getting to know the hot burrito guy who was also a hot wood-carving guy.

"Hi," Ruger greeted. "Are you still up for lunch with me?"

"Of course!" Talli assured him. She suddenly felt reenergized. The mere sight of Ruger had done that—like, replaced her batteries or something. "And congratulations, by the way. I heard you won a couple of the carving events."

Ruger shrugged and said, "Thanks. I hope it helps sales at the auction this afternoon, you know?" Reaching for the backpack Talli was carrying with her extra clothes, he said, "Here, let me carry that for you. If you're as tired as I am, you don't need to be hefting that around too."

"Thanks," Talli said, impressed with his chivalrous, gentlemanly manner. Not that she was surprised. Ruger appeared to be flawless in every other regard, so why shouldn't she have expected he would be so considerate?

"Which Frito pie vendor do you like best?" Ruger asked.

Talli shrugged. "I don't know if I have a favorite. They're all pretty good, right?"

"Yeah," he agreed. "So for the sake that we're both worn out, let's hit the closest one, okay?"

"Sounds like a good plan," Talli giggled.

They started to walk toward the paved pathway that divided funnel cakes from Villarreal's when Ruger unexpectedly stopped in his tracks, saying, "You know what? I gotta do something first."

"Okay," Talli said. She figured he'd forgotten something at the burrito stand and needed to swing by and retrieve it on their way to the nearest Frito pie place.

But when he set her backpack down on the ground and reached out, taking hold of her shoulders—when he said, "Don't freak out, okay?"—Talli simply nodded, rendered breathless by the feel of his strong chainsaw-wielding hands on her shoulders, and breathed, "Okay."

"And please don't think I'm a perv either," Ruger said. He'd lowered his deep, warm voice, and it reminded Talli of honey being drizzled on a sopapilla—and she was the sopapilla being drizzled with it!

"Okay," she breathed. Somehow she already knew what he was thinking. And somehow she wasn't the least bit freaked out—not at all! Although she knew she should be.

It was insane! Talli knew it was. But she sensed the same sort of unbelievable thoughts that were bouncing around inside her head were also bouncing around inside of Ruger's. It was like a scene in a romantic movie, when the main guy and the main girl know the moment they meet that they are meant to be together, that their souls have been looking for one another all their lives. Whether it was because of romantic movies or because something deep inside her heart and soul told her what was about to happen, she knew that Ruger Villarreal was going to kiss her—and only hours after they'd actually met, after only having shared three short conversations.

Therefore, as Ruger's hands slowly moved from her shoulders, as he cautiously gathered her into the power of his muscular arms, Talli was entirely comfortable. In fact, she owned an odd sense of feeling as if she'd been held by him before—as if in his arms were exactly where she belonged. So when he kissed her—when his lips tentatively pressed hers at first once and then again—she allowed her own arms to return his embrace—instinctively kissed him in return. And before Talli could even inhale another full breath, such a delicious passion erupted between her and Ruger that, for a moment, she thought she might explode!

All thoughts of the fact that she hardly knew him were driven from Talli's mind as she kissed Ruger with fully as much desire and fervor as he kissed her! Their mouths mingled perfectly—as if they had been designed to consummately blend only one to the other. Talli's heart swelled with an incredible bliss that she'd never experienced before Ruger had kissed her, and such a feeling of interwoven elation, triumph, satisfaction, and even an odd sort of reprieve so wholly enveloped her that she was certain that Ruger's kiss must be laced with some sort of narcotic! Talli was thoroughgoingly intoxicated by him—by his touch, by the savory, lingering taste of green chile about his mouth. It was true that those who loved green chile to the extent that most native New Mexicans did—to the extent that Talli did—found it utterly addicting, and she wondered if the tinge of green chile in Ruger's kiss was nature's own way of making certain Talli was going to fall for him hook, line, and green-chile sinker!

Slowly Ruger lessened the intensity of their kisses, until much too soon their mouths separated altogether and they were left gazing into one another's eyes, as understanding and tentative acceptance of what was meant to be settled over them.

"Damn, girl!" Ruger mumbled, grinning and brushing a strand of stray hair from Talli's forehead. "It is you."

Talli smiled—giggled a little in being so intoxicatingly happy that Ruger was feeling and thinking the same things she had been.

"So?" she ventured. "What do we do now?"

Flashing a dazzling smile that literally caused Talli's knees to go weak, Ruger said, "We grab some Frito pie and have our first lunch together."

"Okay," Talli said, every inch of her being erupting with goose bumps as Ruger did not pause in putting his arm around her shoulders and pulling her snugly under his arm. Picking up her backpack with his free hand, he slung it over his shoulder, and they began walking.

"Órale, vato! Already?" Colt Villarreal called with a chuckle as Ruger and Talli walked past his breakfast burrito stand.

"Already?" Ruger laughed. "It's been five years in the making, bro!"

Colt winked at Talli, tossed an approving chin-thrust at her, and said, "Welcome to the family, funnel cake girl!"

Talli blushed and returned Colt's wink as Ruger pressed a quick kiss to her temple.

"Don't wake up, don't wake up…" she whispered quietly to herself.

"What?" Ruger asked.

"Oh, nothing," Talli said, smiling up at him.

Inhaling a deep breath, Talli exhaled it slowly, savoring every scent and aroma she could. For she knew it was a day she would never forget, and she wanted to remember every detail of it that she could—always.

CHAPTER FIVE

"Sooo…you're a chainsaw carver?" Talli asked as she and Ruger stood in line at the Frito pie stand. She still couldn't believe he'd kissed her—couldn't believe she was having lunch with him—couldn't believe he was something as sexy and manly as a chainsaw wood-carver—couldn't believe any of it! Yet there she stood, right next to him, waiting to order lunch with him. She felt a wave of dizziness wash over her, but it subsided quickly, and she made a mental note to remember to drink a ton of water when she got home. She was really bad at remembering to drink enough water when she was working the fiesta—and she was sure it was the reason she had felt a little dizzy.

"Yep," Ruger said with an emphatic nod of confirmation, "except for the one week a year when I'm a burrito stand guy."

Talli smiled. "But even while you're the burrito stand guy, you're a chainsaw wood-carving guy on your breaks, so you're still a chainsaw wood-carver…even for this week."

A low chuckle emanated from Ruger's throat. "I guess you're right," he noted. "And being that I do sell a lot of pieces at the fiesta, I guess I'm doing double duty this week. And here I always thought of it as a vacation from my everyday job."

"But in truth, you're only moonlighting," Talli pointed out, smiling at him. "As for me, I have to take the entire week off to work the funnel cake place. It wears me out! There's no way I could do this and my regular job. I'd be worthless for a month afterward."

Ruger grinned as he looked at her, and Talli could've sworn the light green of his eyes deepened a shade as he did so. His rather smoldering gaze caused butterflies to begin fluttering in her stomach again—just being looked at by him caused it! And when again she thought of his kissing her—of the fabulous, wonderful, magnificent, perfect kiss only minutes before—Talli felt her knees weaken.

"And your regular job is…" he prodded.

"Well, it's nothing as exciting and unique as a chainsaw wood-carver, but I enjoy it all the same," she began. "I'm an esthetician."

"Oh…so you ride horses and stuff?" Ruger offered.

When Talli looked at him in amused surprise, he tossed a chin-thrust her way, smiled, and said, "I'm just kidding. I know what an esthetician is."

"You do?" Talli asked, surprised. Since becoming a fully licensed esthetician and working at the spa, as well as part-time for Dr. Fillmore at his dermatology center, Talli had discovered most of the general public didn't fully understand what an esthetician was—not exactly.

"Sure," Ruger said as he and Talli moved forward a couple of steps in unison as the line moved. "You work on people's face skin, right? Creams, wax eyebrows, stuff like that."

"Well, yes, that's part of it," Talli confirmed, impressed that Ruger—a chainsaw-wielding manly man—knew something about estheticians.

"Hey wait!" he exclaimed unexpectedly. Turning to face her, he took her shoulders between his rugged, callused, very powerful hands and said, "You're also like that pimple popping lady online, right? Don't estheticians sometimes do blackheads and acne and stuff? I love those videos. They intrigue me and gross me out at the same time." He was smiling with complete sincerity.

"You...you watch those, like, blackhead and cyst-popping videos?" Talli asked, still astonished that Ruger knew anything at all about estheticians.

"Oh yeah, all the time," Ruger freely admitted without a moment's pause.

Again Talli stepped forward in unison with Ruger. There was only one person in line in front of them now. Therefore, and understandably, Ruger's attention was drawn away from talk of their individual careers and to the menu board above the order counter.

"I'm starving," he mumbled. "I'm going for the works. You?"

Talli studied the menu board as well, and being that her stomach was complaining that it was empty too, she nodded, agreeing, "Yeah, me too."

"I can help you over here," a young woman said as she stepped up to the ordering counter, removing the This Window Closed sign in front of her.

"Great, thanks," Ruger said, taking hold of Talli's hand and leading her toward the newly opened window.

Talli did not miss how the young woman's face lit up with a delighted blush and pleased smile as Ruger came to stand before her on his side of the counter.

"What can I do for you today, sir?" the pretty young woman asked—the pretty young woman with long blue-black hair and olive skin so pristinely smooth and beautiful that Talli felt her heart twinge with worry that Ruger would be suddenly so taken by the beautiful Frito pie girl that he'd forget about Talli altogether.

"Can I get two with everything?" Ruger asked, however, still studying the menu.

"Of course," the girl said, smiling alluringly at Ruger.

Talli began to wonder, for the first time since he'd kissed her, if maybe it was only the magic of the balloon fiesta that had Ruger thinking he wanted to have Talli as his own—and not something deeper.

"Anything to drink?" the girl asked him.

"Um…" Ruger looked to Talli again, asking, "What do you want to drink?"

"Just water would be great," Talli answered.

"Yeah, two waters," Ruger said.

And then it happened. As the Frito pie girl stood grinning at Ruger like an abandoned puppy who'd just been adopted by the boy of her dreams, Talli heard both her own voice and Ruger's simultaneously chime, "And can I get a side of green chile, please?"

As Talli looked to Ruger, Ruger looked to Talli, and again it happened. "How funny," they both exclaimed in unison.

"I always get extra green chile," Ruger noted, grinning.

"As do I," Talli giggled.

Reaching out and caressing Talli's cheek with the back of his hand, Ruger said, "You see? It's meant to be, you and me."

His touch sent goose bumps racing over her arms and legs—up the back of her neck—and for a moment, Talli considered asking Ruger if this was a rehearsed ruse he used with women—pretending that he'd found "the one" with them in order to position them right where he wanted them. Yet the smoldering emerald of his fascinating eyes radiated sincerity, not pretense.

"Two everythings with two sides of green chile and two waters then? Is that it?" the pretty Frito pie girl asked.

"Yep. For now anyway," Ruger affirmed.

"All right. That will be twenty-five dollars even," the Frito pie girl said. "And the name?"

"Ruger," Ruger answered, retrieving his wallet from his back right pocket.

Ruger still had Talli's backpack hooked over one broad shoulder. Quickly she unzipped the small front pocket and began digging for her cash.

"Hold on, I've got cash for mine," she said.

"Ah ah ah," Ruger playfully argued, however, wrenching his shoulder back so that the backpack slipped out of Talli's hands. "I've got this."

"B-but I already mooched free burritos off you today and—" Talli began.

"You swapped me for some funnel cakes, remember?" he pointed out. "Remind me to pick those up and take them over to Colt and everyone when we're finished with lunch, by the way."

"Yeah, but—" Talli stammered.

"Nope." Ruger said as he handed the Frito pie girl a twenty and a ten. "No Dutch treating when you're with me, girl."

"Well, thanks…although I feel really bad. I mean, I ruined your apron with my bloody chin, bummed free burritos off you, and now you're paying for my lunch. I don't want you to think I'm trying to take advantage of you or anything."

As the pretty Frito pie girl handed a five dollar bill to Ruger as his change—as Ruger stuffed the five dollar bill into the plastic jar on the counter with a "Tips Appreciated" sign taped to it—Ruger smiled a very mischievous smile at Talli, winked at her, and said, "Oh, you feel free to take advantage of me any time and in any way you want to, querida."

Talli's heart leapt with delight! Oh sure, maybe Ruger had simply watched a ton of reruns of the old black-and-white TV series The Addams Family when he was a kid and thought Gomez Addams's flirting with his wife, Morticia, by calling her querida was funny. But Talli decided to go with her first instinct—that Ruger Villarreal really knew that querida translated to "my darling" and had meant to call her that.

The Frito pie girl giggled with charmed amusement. Talli looked from Ruger to the Frito pie girl to see her nod toward Talli in a silent gesture of, I get it. He's taken…and you're one lucky woman! as she jotted Ruger's name on an order slip.

"We'll have that right up for you," the girl said, smiling. "Just step over to the order pickup window. It won't be long."

"Thanks," Ruger thanked her with a nod.

As Ruger and Talli stepped over to stand in the pickup line, he again mumbled, "I'm not kidding. I'm starving."

"Well, I can imagine that you are! After all that manly chainsawing and winning all those contests," Talli teased. "It must work up quite an appetite."

"It does," he said, winking at her again. He shrugged broad, broad, super broad shoulders, adding, "You'd think neither one of us would be hungry, considering where we worked this morning, right?"

"I know, huh?" Talli agreed. "Still, funnel cake ain't Frito pie."

"Neither are breakfast burritos," Ruger noted.

There was silence between them then—too much silence for Talli's comfort. She began to worry, wondering what she would do if the silence continued. After all the long, lingering looks she and Ruger had shared throughout the day—after the kiss from the City of Ecstasy Ruger had planted on her behind the funnel cake stand—what if he'd changed his mind about her? What if they had nothing to talk about? What if the daydreaming over him for five balloon fiestas in a row turned out to be nothing but unrequited daydreaming?

"Wanna grab some napkins and forks?" Ruger asked as a guy came to the order counter carrying a tray with two heaping Frito pies and two waters.

"Sure," Talli said. She stepped up to one side of the window, grabbed two forks out of the basket full of utensils sitting on the counter, and then began gathering a few napkins. At this point in the fiesta, vendors were generous, leaving utensils and napkins outside their food stands for patrons to load up on. Talli knew that as the fiesta continued, all the vendors, including the funnel cake stand, wouldn't be so willing to offer such a volume of free supplies.

"Ruger?" she heard the guy at the window call.

"That's me," she heard Ruger say. "Thanks, man."

Turning around, she smiled as Ruger lifted one large Styrofoam bowl heaping with Frito pie from the tray, handing it to her.

"Oh, thanks!" she said, shoving the napkins and forks into the front pocket of her jeans before accepting the bowl.

"I've got the rest," Ruger said, taking the two bottled waters and two sealable bags of roasted green chile from the tray in one large, capable hand and the second bowl of Frito pie in the other. "Let's find a spot. You wanna try and find a table? Or just sit in the grass?"

"I like the grass best. You?" Talli answered and asked.

Ruger smiled with obvious approval of her choice. "Me too," he said.

Together they headed away from Vendors' Row and toward the grassy balloon field itself. Many patrons had already staked claims amid the lush, green grass of the field and were either picnicking from their own coolers or enjoying food from the various vendors.

"Tell me when," Talli said as she headed toward the very center of the field.

"Oh, just find a place out here in the middle somewhere," Ruger instructed.

A few moments more and Talli stopped in a warm, sunny spot on the field. "This okay?"

"Perfect," Ruger affirmed. Glancing around the grassy area, he said, "I should've grabbed something for us to set our food on, at least."

"Wait," Talli said. Balancing the bowl of Frito pie in her left hand, she moved to where her backpack hung from Ruger's broad shoulder. Unzipping the pack's main compartment, she pulled out her black sweatshirt, tossing it to the ground and then kneeling down and spreading it out across the grass.

"Here you go," she said, placing her bowl of Frito pie on the sweatshirt and then reaching up to take Ruger's as he handed it to her. "This will be just perfect! And the dew is all gone from the grass so we won't get wet. We're all good!"

Ruger nodded and sat down next to Talli. He handed her a water and one of the baggies of green chile. "Now this is living, right?" he asked, exhaling a long sigh of contentment.

"Absolutely!" Talli agreed with a delighted giggle. "There's nothing like lounging in the grass of the balloon field and eating two thousand calories in one bowl!"

Talli removed the plastic utensils and napkins from her front pocket and handed a set to Ruger. "So I've always wondered," she began as she twisted the cap off her bottle of water.

"Yeah?" Ruger asked as he did the same.

"Is it Frito pie?" she asked. "You know, like named after the fact that there are actual Frito-Lay Fritos in the bottom of the bowl? Or is it frijto pie…like meaning fried pie, the fried coming from the fact that some people make it with tortilla chips?"

Ruger smiled, shrugging his broad shoulders. "I have no idea," he admitted. "Although, you're right. I've heard it called Frito pie when it's served with tortilla chips too. I never thought about that before. Though I will say that, in my opinion, it's not real Frito pie unless it has Frito corn chips in the bottom, you know?"

"I agree," Talli said a moment before she took a bite of the piping hot deliciousness in her bowl. "Mmm!" she moaned. "I was way more hungry than I thought, I guess."

"Me too," Ruger agreed, already on his second bite of Frito pie.

Talli loved Frito pie! Especially at the balloon fiesta or the New Mexico State Fair. To her, it seemed the Fritos were crunchier, the chili spicier, the grated cheese fresher, and the tomatoes tasting closer to the homegrown ones she remembered from her grandmother's garden, rather than the bred-to-travel kind in the grocery stores.

Ruger finished chewing and swallowing his mouthful of Frito pie and then said, "You know, I've always thought this sweatshirt of yours was pretty funny. Dracula sucks…so funny."

Talli smiled as she chewed. Waiting until she'd swallowed her own bite of lunch, she offered, "Yep. It was my mom's. She made it when my brother was really little, and she wore it every Halloween when our family went trick-or-treating. I guess she thought that, after we were all too old to trick-or-treat, the fun was over…so she retired it. I found it in the back of her closet one year and asked her if I could have it to wear to the fiesta." Talli shrugged, adding, "I don't know. It just always makes me feel warm by reminding me of those fun Halloweens when I was little." She paused, realizing exactly what Ruger had said. "What do you mean, you've always thought it was funny?"

"I mean always," he answered. "Ever since I first saw you wearing it years ago."

Talli blushed with pleasure in knowing he'd truly noticed exactly what she'd been wearing to the fiesta all these years. "You noticed my sweatshirt?"

"Yep," Ruger confirmed. "I look forward to watching you strip every year too."

"What?" Talli laughed.

Ruger smiled, glad he'd made her laugh. "You know…you show up wearing the Dracula sweatshirt, and then pretty soon you strip it off to reveal that long-sleeved Nebraska T-shirt you wear, and eventually you strip that off and you're down to that white t-shirt you're wearing right now." His smile broadened, and he winked at her. "You didn't know I was watching you strip all this time, did you?"

Blushing tomato red, Talli shook her head, saying, "No! I certainly did not!"

"It's the highlight of the balloon fiesta for me," Ruger teased. "Freaking Colt had me working so hard this morning, I almost missed the transition from the Nebraska shirt to the white T-shirt. That would've been devastating!"

"Oh, I'm sure," Talli said, still blushing and shaking her head again.

"I'm serious," Ruger assured her, however. "If there's one thing you'll come to know about me, I'm a diehard traditionalist."

"A traditionalist, huh?" Talli asked, quirking one eyebrow with doubt. "I never knew traditionalists were so…so…spontaneous."

Ruger stopped eating for a moment, leaning closer to her. Talli felt her heart begin to race at his nearness—at the mischief smoldering in his gorgeous green eyes.

"You're referring to my kissing you before lunch, right?" he teased.

Talli blushed—for the kiss was indeed exactly what she was referring to. "Well, y-yes," she admitted as he stared at her—grinning.

Ruger shrugged. "What? Aren't traditionalists allowed to be spontaneous too?"

"I-I-I guess," Talli answered.

"I freaked you out, didn't I?" Ruger asked, still grinning.

Blushing so deeply she could feel it spreading to her ears, Talli answered, "No...not really. I mean, I was surprised...but not freaked out."

"Pleasantly surprised?" Ruger asked, winking at her.

"Admittedly...yes."

Ruger's handsome smile broadened with either pride or relief—Talli wasn't sure which. Either way, it whisked away her rational thought so that when Ruger said, "Well, it wasn't like we haven't been building up to it, right? I mean, we've been stare-dating for, like, five years now. So I think it's about time we quit pussy-footin' around and got down to business, don't you?"

"Stare-dating? Pussy-footin'?" Talli asked, giggling.

"Yeah!" Ruger assured her. "You know, staring at each other across the entrance to the park all the time, hoping we wouldn't get caught by each other. And this year...well, divine intervention finally stepped up and tripped you going down the hill into the park, and we were finally forced to speak to each other."

He reached out, gently caressing the scrape on her chin with his thumb. "I'm just sorry it was a painful first conversation with me for you."

As goose bumps broke over her arms and legs again—as her entire face felt overly warm from the simple touch of his thumb—Talli said, "It was worth it."

Ruger smiled, chuckling, "I sure hope so. That was quite the impressive tumble you took this morning. How could I resist trying to trap you in my net by kissing you, huh? I mean, after watching you strip for the fifth year in a row...I couldn't control myself any longer."

Talli laughed and watched Ruger pull a roasted green chile from his bag.

"You don't even know me," she stated. "I mean...not really. Other than what I wear every morning for one week out of the year. How can you...I mean..."

Again Ruger shrugged. "I just know. I can't explain it to you. I mean, how do you feel, Talli Chaucer? If I asked you to marry me right now, right this minute, what would your answer be?"

Talli could hardly draw a breath. He had to be kidding! He had to be!

"You're kidding me, right?" she asked.

"Nope," Ruger answered firmly. "I mean, I'm not asking you...not right this minute anyway. But if I were to ask you, right this minute...what would your instincts tell you to answer?"

Talli wanted to believe him—wanted to believe that the gorgeous, hot, super sexy burrito guy she'd been goo-goo over for the past five years was sincere, but it seemed too surreal—totally impossible.

"I'm not a player, Talli," Ruger said, his expression that of profound sincerity. "You might think I'm crazy, but the first time I saw you years ago, my first thought—and I'm not kidding—my first thought was, I wonder how long I have to wait for her to be old enough to marry me? I'm serious."

Talli could see that he was. Yet it couldn't be that easy. It couldn't! A girl just didn't stroll into balloon fiesta park one morning and have the man of her dreams—her five long years of dreams—walk up to her, kiss her, and tell her that someday he was going to ask her to marry him. It just didn't happen that way! Especially when the guy of her dreams looked like Ruger Villarreal did! Right?

"So," he began. His voice dropped to a low, serious tone as he continued, "I've laid my cards on the table. Are you willing to show me your hand?"

Reaching out, Ruger cupped her chin in one strong hand. Pressing a soft yet very titillating kiss to her lips, he asked, "If I asked you right now…what would you say? Don't think about what other people would think—not parents, siblings, friends. Just tell me what your gut would tell you to say."

Again he kissed her, this time more firmly—and over and over again. And she kissed him back each and every time.

"I'd say yes," she admitted in a whisper.

"And there you go," Ruger said, grinning at her with understanding and affirmation. "If we're both feeling the same thing, then it doesn't matter what anyone else says. We'll just go forward at our own pace…whether it's slow or fast. Okay?"

The deep sincerity in his eyes gave her courage. Ruger meant what he was saying. As insane as it sounded, he meant it. And though she still struggled to believe it, it was there right before her—the truth. Ruger Villarreal had had the same thought the moment he'd seen her five years before that she'd had the moment she'd seen him—that they were meant for each other!

Ruger kissed her, and Talli sighed with delight as she tasted the unique and wonderful flavor of green chile in his kiss.

"Híjole, bro! You do move fast!"

Ruger's brother's voice caused Talli to feel shy and uncomfortable, and she pulled away from him, ending their kiss.

"Dude!" Ruger scolded, frowning at his brother. "You can't see that I'm wooing my woman right now, or what?"

"But, bro," Colt continued with excitement, "you just sold that elk carving…the twenty thousand dollar one, bro! I just saw them put a sold sign on it."

"No way!" Ruger exclaimed. "Already?"

"Yeah, man! I just came from there!" Colt assured his brother. "Day one and you're already making bank!" Colt's smile broadened as he looked at Talli and winked. "My boy's gonna be able to sweep you off your feet in style now, chica!"

Ruger smiled and nodded. "Damn right!" he laughed, exchanging knuckle bumps with his brother.

Talli blushed—blushed even harder when Colt said, "Don't be bashful, girl. I know my bro, and if he's after you this hard…girl, he's serious! Now finish your lunch, vato," Colt said. "You should probably go over there and schmooze the buyer before he leaves, que no?"

"Yeah, I'll run over there when we're finished with lunch and I see Talli back to her car," Ruger assured his brother.

Colt tossed a chin-thrust to Ruger and said, "Okay, bro. Let me know what they say." He looked at Talli then, adding, "Welcome to the family, chica." Leveling a playful index finger at her, Colt said, "And don't forget to bring me a funnel cake before you leave today, right?"

"I won't," Talli assured him, smiling.

She was astonished at how easily—at how quickly—Colt had accepted the fact that Ruger seemed so serious about a girl he'd only just met. Yet it was obvious Ruger was close to his brother.

Therefore, Talli figured they were like any other set of very close siblings, wherein they could read each other like books.

"Later, eses," Colt said. He paused before leaving, smiled, lowered his voice, and added to Ruger, "And, bro, take that woman to the RV to make out, man! This ain't comfortable for her out here on the field. Eee! Didn't I teach you nothing?"

Colt tossed a chin-thrust to Ruger and Talli and then turned to leave.

"You sold a carving for twenty thousand dollars? Is he kidding?" Talli asked.

But Ruger shook his head as he stuffed another roasted green chile into his mouth, followed by a big bite of Frito pie. "Nope. I make a good chunk of my annual salary here at the fiesta," he explained. "And that elk piece..." He shook his head in apparent amazement. "I wasn't sure it would sell at all. It's not my favorite."

All at once, Talli put two and two together. "The big, big, big beautiful wood carving of the bull and cow elk...is yours?" she exclaimed. "I-I-I saw that when I was walking back to the funnel cake stand after watching you carve today. That's yours?"

"Yeah," Ruger said casually—as if the incredible wood sculpture was no more than a Play-Doh sculpture he'd made in kindergarten class. "But like I said...it's not one of my favorites here this year. So I'm actually surprised it sold this soon. Glad, but surprised."

"Well, you certainly should go talk to the buyer," Talli encouraged. "I mean, repeat business...that's what every artist wants, right?"

Ruger smiled at her, took another bite of Frito pie, and nodded with pleased approval. "Yes, that's exactly what every artist wants. And thanks for calling me an artist, by the way. Mostly I'm just a guy who whacks out statues from logs, you know."

"I'm serious," Talli said. "You really should go talk to that buyer."

"What? Now?" Ruger asked, frowning. "We're having lunch together. The buyer can wait."

Talli smiled, deliciously flattered that he was choosing to stay with her rather than go network his business.

"You know what? I really want you to go talk to your buyer. I'll worry if you don't," she confessed.

Ruger paused, frowning a bit. "But…I don't want to go right now."

"Well, are we still going to Dion's for dinner?" Talli asked, hopeful.

Ruger smiled. "Of course we are!"

"Then I'll just go home, take a little nap so I can think coherently tonight at dinner, and you can schmooze your buyer, okay?" she suggested. "I mean, I don't want to ruin my reputation with you as a sexy stripper, but I feel kind of grimy after frying funnel cake all morning, you know?"

Ruger chuckled. "Oh, you mean you want to slip into something more comfortable before I pick you up for dinner tonight?"

Talli blushed and giggled. "Yep. That's exactly it."

"Well, let me at least walk you to your car and see that you—" Ruger began.

"Nope," Talli interrupted. "My friend Cata should be driving the golf car shuttles up and down the hill by now. I'll just catch a ride with her and head home."

"But I don't feel good about letting you go by yourself," Ruger said, frowning.

How adorable was he? How charming? How gentlemanly? Talli was over the moon with elation at his attempts at pampering her!

And yet she knew other artists and vendors at the fiesta and therefore knew how important pampering buyers and networking was. Anyone who had that kind of money to lay out on one carving probably had deeper pockets and would be willing to buy more at some future point.

Therefore, she said, "Seriously, Ruger. I'm way, way tired. I need a good nap, and you need to network. I'm a strong girl. I can get to my car by myself."

Ruger, still frowning, said, "Well, I don't really want you to—"

"Twenty thousand dollars, Ruger. The guy spent twenty thousand dollars on one sculpture," she reminded him.

Reaching into the front pocket of his jeans, he withdrew his cell phone. "Okay, I guess I can let it slide this one time. But put your number in my phone first so I can call you and get your address so I can pick you up. Okay?"

Talli smiled as he handed her his phone. "Okay. Where do you live, by the way?" she inquired as she entered her number into his phone.

"On the west side," he answered. "And text yourself so you'll have my number, okay?"

"Of course," Talli assured him. "After all, I want to send you stalking text messages if you don't show up tonight."

She gasped, surprised when Ruger reached out, and took her chin in one hand. "Not funny. You know I'm legit, right?" His eyes were narrowed with severity—intensity in needing to know she trusted him.

"I know," she said, sighing when he kissed her quickly.

"Would around six tonight be okay?" he asked, stuffing his phone back in his jeans pocket when she was finished with it. "And you should probably text me your address too."

"I live on the west side, as well," she answered. "And six would be great." Talli frowned then; she couldn't help it. "But…can I ask you one thing?" she asked.

"Of course," Ruger said, stuffing the rest of his side of green chile into his mouth. Talli smiled, for she could see that now that he'd decided to go ahead and schmooze the buyer of the elk sculpture, he was anxious to do so.

"You don't always carry your cell in your front pocket, do you?" she ventured.

"No," Ruger answered. "But why do you ask?"

Talli shook her head, quickly wishing she hadn't said anything. "Oh, I was just…just wondering. You know, with all this talk about cell phones causing cancer and things…I just wondered…"

Unexpectedly Ruger laughed out loud, leaned forward, and kissed Talli again. "Awesome! We've been a couple for all of forty-five minutes and you're already worried about my testicles!"

Blushing to the tips of her toes as several people sitting nearby turned to stare at her, Talli stammered, "No, no, no. I'm worried about you—all of you—not just your…your…"

"My testicles," Ruger finished for her, grinning in knowing he'd embarrassed her.

"No! All of you!" Talli insisted, turning as red as her grandmother's summer tomatoes.

"But you asked me if I always carry it in my front pocket because you're worried about the health and well-being of my testicles…admit it," Ruger chuckled.

"If you'll stop shouting testicles over and over, yes…I'll admit it," Talli confessed. "I mean, they say women shouldn't carry their phones in their bras and that men shouldn't carry them in their front pockets…because of the increased risk of breast cancer as well as…as…"

"Testicular cancer," Ruger finished for her.

Exhaling a heavy sigh of defeat, Talli nodded. "Exactly."

"Well then, not to worry, querida," Ruger said, caressing her cheek with the back of his hand. "I hardly ever carry my phone in my front pocket near my—"

"Don't say it!" Talli giggled.

Ruger smiled at her again—kissed her again. "It's going to be fun…me and you getting to know each other better and better, no?"

"Yes," Talli admitted, momentarily intoxicated by the expression of admiration on his face as he stared at her.

"Well, I better get over there and meet this new patron of the chainsaw wood-carving arts, right?" he asked.

"I think you should, yes," Talli agreed.

"Six o'clock then?" Ruger asked.

"Perfect," Talli assured him.

"And you're sure your friend can take you up the hill to your car?" he asked.

"I'm sure," Talli giggled. "And I'll pick up our lunch stuff. You just go before that buyer gets away."

"Okay," Ruger halfheartedly agreed. "See you at six-ish."

"I honestly can't wait," Talli admitted.

Ruger smiled, winked at her, and said, "Me neither. You have no idea, girl."

"Oh, I think I do," Talli said.

Ruger winked again and said, "Okay, bye."

"Bye," Talli said. "Now go."

Ruger nodded, stood, and started jogging toward the wood-carving area.

Talli watched him go—admired the way he moved as he jogged—her heart doing flip-flops inside her chest as she thought of his kiss. The sexy burrito guy had kissed her! More than that, he'd practically proposed to her!

Gathering up the remains of their lunch, Talli shoved a couple of green chiles from her own bag into her mouth.

"Mmmm!" she moaned as she headed toward the nearest garbage can. Tossing the trash into the garbage can at the edge of Vendors' Row, Talli slung her backpack over one shoulder and started up the paved hill toward the parking log. "Oh shoot!" Talli mumbled, realizing she had again neglected to take a few funnel cakes to Colt at the Villarreal's burrito stand. Retrieving her phone from her backpack, she quickly texted Rosie and asked her to.

"Hey, girl! Are you finally done for today?" Cata asked as she pulled up next to Talli in a golf cart.

"I am!" Talli answered as she read Rosie's responding text promising she would deliver the funnel cakes to Colt. "And I'm worn out, girl!"

"Well, hop on! I'm on my way up, and you do look wrung out," Cata offered.

Talli hopped into the front passenger's seat of the cart, and Cata hit the gas.

"Anything exciting happen at the funnel cake stand today?" Cata asked.

Talli sighed and smiled as a feeling of warm felicity began to wash over her. "You wouldn't believe me if I told you," she answered.

"Eee, girl! Now you have to tell me!" Cata insisted.

Talli laughed. Even as the familiar feeling of thoroughgoing fatigue began to wash over her—the kind of fatigue she only experienced one week a year, the kind that would find her showered and crashed out on her bed as soon as she made it home—she laughed.

The brilliant New Mexico sun was warm and relaxing as she rode with Cata up the hill, quickly explaining some of what had happened with Ruger. In truth, she only told her friend about her fall that morning in front of the sexy burrito guy and the fact that he'd asked her to lunch. She kept the rest of the wondrous miracle to herself. For after all, no matter what Ruger said, people would think they'd both lost their minds—or at the very least, that someone had sprinkled crack on their funnel cake instead of powdered sugar.

CHAPTER SIX

As Ruger drove his black Dodge Ram down Unser Boulevard on his way to pick up Talli, a million thoughts competed for his full attention. First and foremost were his thoughts of Talli—of how wonderful she was, how pretty, how soft her lips were, how her smile made his stomach begin churning with excitement. He worried as well; had he shown his hand too soon? Even though she appeared to be on the same page with him—knowing they were meant for each other—he still wondered if he'd pressed her too hard. After all, he'd kissed her right out of the gate! Not that she'd seemed to mind. She'd kissed him back full as wantonly as he'd kissed her. In fact, she'd kissed him back every time he'd kissed her—even the short, quick kisses he'd given her during their luncheon on the balloon field. But that old devil, doubt—it was a powerful thing, and it kept pricking his brain, even for Ruger's determination to ignore it.

He'd made a killing on the first day of the fiesta! So far—and there was still the balloon glow that night to bring in potential customers—Ruger had netted over fifty grand on opening day! It was a great start to what he hoped would continue to be a lucrative week.

His Bluetooth kicked on, and Ruger winced as he answered. "Hi, Nineteen-Eleven."

"Hi, Ruger," his sister's voice greeted. "What's up?"

"Not much," Ruger said, hoping his sister (named after one of his father's favorite firearms, the American-made Kimber 1911 pistol) was just calling to see if he'd sold any pieces at the fiesta that day. Momentarily, the thought traveled through Ruger's mind that his parents had really hit the nail on the head when they'd named Kimber. After all, her personality was nothing short of having the same power and precision of the .45-caliber Kimber 1911 chosen by the LAPD SWAT and Marine Corp Special Ops Command. No one could take Kimber Villarreal down if she planted her feet determinedly—no matter what the situation or subject.

"Well, that's not what I hear," Kimber said, causing Ruger to wince once more.

"Oh, you mean the fact that the elk sculpture sold today?" Ruger offered, again hoping that it was the reason Kimber was calling—though his intuition told him differently.

"Um…I did hear that, yes," Kimber answered. "But I'm talking about this girl you were apparently making out with on the balloon field around noon or so. What's that all about?"

"We weren't making out, Kimber," Ruger began. "Man! Does Colt have a big mouth or what?"

"It wasn't Colt that told me," Kimber countered. "It was Sophia. She saw you kissing some strange girl. So who was she?"

Ruger rolled his eyes with exasperation. Sophia Montoya had been a pain in his neck for years! Ruger had dated her briefly in college—very briefly. But unfortunately very briefly was all had taken for Sophia to become somewhat obsessed that Ruger hadn't fallen madly in love with her and also to become fast friends with Kimber. Sophia had been a fly in the ointment ever since. Of all the people in the world, Ruger thought, why did it have to be Sophia Montoya to see him with Talli?

"She's not a strange girl," Ruger answered almost curtly. "Her name is Talli, and I'm on my way to pick her up right now. In fact..."

"Talli?" Kimber exclaimed with obvious disapproval. "What kind of a name is Talli? And why don't I know her? If you're already making out with her in public, you could've at least had the decency to introduce me to her first."

"First of all, Talli is a cute name for a beautiful woman," Ruger nearly growled. No one got his dander up like his older sister. "Second of all, I don't need your approval to kiss her or to date her, Kimber. So take it down a notch if you don't want me to hang up. I like this girl. I like her a lot! And she's the one, so you better just start accepting it now."

"The one?" Kimber rather screeched. "Ruger...have you lost your mind? How do you know she's the one? I'd never even heard of her before Sophia told me she saw you with her today! Sounds to me like you're not thinking with your brain. Sounds to me like you're thinking more with your—"

Tapping his Bluetooth, Ruger hung up on his sister. His feelings for Talli were none of her damn business. Besides, he didn't want her ruining his mood. He was going to enjoy having dinner with Talli at Dion's. He'd deal with Kimber later. Exhaling a heavy sigh of frustration with the sister he loved so much—but who could also get way too bossy ninety percent of the time—Ruger went back to thinking about Talli.

He was very familiar with the neighborhood she lived in, being that Colt lived nearby, and felt his heart leap in his chest when he turned onto her street. In just a few minutes, she'd be in the truck with him, and they'd be on their way—on their way to permanently being together. He had no doubt of that. No matter what Kimber thought.

♥

"Ruger, huh?" Talli's dad said for the umpteen-millionth time.

"Yes, Daddy. Ruger," Talli told him with a giggle. "Give it a rest, will you?"

"Well, it's just a weird name, that's all," Brent Chaucer mumbled.

"As opposed to Talli?" Talli teased.

Her father smiled and winked at her from his place eating a bowl of Frosted Flakes at the kitchen table.

"Talli pointed him out to me last year at the balloon fiesta, honey," Alicia Chaucer mumbled. "And as her mom, I totally approve! This Ruger is a handsome guy! And when he waited on me last year at the breakfast burrito place, he was very charming and polite." Alicia smiled at her daughter from her place at the stove, where she stood stirring a caramel mixture for the batch of caramel corn she was making. "And Talli has always had good judgment where boys are concerned. So you need to stop worrying, Brent."

"Well, sure," Brent agreed. "Talli has always had good judgment where boys are concerned. But this guy sounds like a grown, chainsaw-wielding man. And that's a long way from bubblegum and boys."

"Oh, just eat your cereal," Alicia said, smiling and shaking her head with amusement. "I'm sure he's a great guy."

Talli knew her dad was simply being overdramatic. But she hoped he'd tone it down once Ruger had arrived. Her dad would more often than not tease someone incessantly, and she knew Ruger—being that he was coming to pick her up to go out for the first time—might as well arrive with a target painted on his forehead where her dad's razzing was concerned.

Talli's dad was intimidating in his own right. He wasn't the average middle-aged man. Nope. Brent Chaucer was tall, in great physical condition, and had accepted his thinning hair a few years before by going with what Talli referred to as "The Transporter" look—short-cropped hair, buzzed to about a quarter of an inch or less. Her dad claimed that once a man's hair was gone, he needed to man up and admit it. And buzzing it down to near nothing, like Jason Statham (the actor in the original Transporter movies), was the best option. No comb-overs, no razor-shaving one's scalp—just buzz it short and keep oneself in great physical condition. And that's exactly what Brent Chaucer did. Talli was secretly very proud of her handsome, muscly dad. Furthermore, her two older brothers, both of whom were law enforcement officers, still couldn't take her dad down more than two out of ten times while wrestling in the family room. Yep, Brent Chaucer was a wonderful man to call Dad. But Talli still hoped her father would go easy on the teasing when Ruger arrived.

She hadn't told her parents everything about Ruger—certainly not! After all, any set of parents would completely freak out if their daughter came home one day and said, I met the man of my dreams today, and we've pretty much already talked about getting married. Naturally, her mother knew about Ruger—had known about the hot guy that worked at the breakfast burrito stand ever since the first balloon fiesta Talli had worked the funnel cake stand. And yes, she had pointed out said hot guy to her mother one morning the year before when her parents were at the fiesta. It was one thing she adored about her mother—appreciated as well—the fact that Talli had always been able to confide in her mom about her various crushes and infatuations throughout her life. Talli's mom understood the heart of a young girl, a teenager girl, and a young woman. Her mother never made light of their quiet conversations about boys and had always given Talli wise, insightful advice in matters of the heart. Still, Talli wasn't ready to drop the whole payload of the Ruger bomb—even on her mom. Not yet. She figured it would be smart to at least go on one official date with Ruger before talking to her mom about the depth of her feelings for him.

The doorbell rang, and Talli startled a little. Her heart began to pound double-time in her chest, and she said, "Now, Dad...please don't be too weird, okay?"

Brent Chaucer looked up from his bowl of Frosted Flakes. "Me? Weird? When have I ever been weird around one of your dates, hmm?"

Talli playfully glared at her dad for a moment—until he said, "Okay, okay. I won't be weird."

"Thank you," she sighed.

"Ooo! Let me answer the door, Talls. I want to get a closer look at this guy," Alicia Chaucer giggled.

"You'll scorch the caramel for the popcorn," Brent offered.

"Oh, it's boiling, and it still needs a minute or two. It'll be fine," Alicia assured him, wiping her hands on her apron and hurrying out of the kitchen and toward the entryway and front door.

"Mom! Don't be weird!" Talli scolded in a whisper as she hurried after her mother.

But her mother beat her to the front door and quickly opened it, greeting, "Well, hello! I'm Talli's weird mother, Alicia Chaucer. Won't you come in, Mr. Villarreal?"

Talli was wishing she'd warned her mother not to be weird in front of Ruger before warning her father, but as Ruger Villarreal stepped over the threshold and into the house, Talli's mouth dropped open a moment in dazzled awe. Ruger was awe-inspiring!

Not that he looked any different than he had at the fiesta earlier that day. But seeing him there, standing right there in her own home—dressed in jeans, boots, and a red fitted T-shirt—he had literally taken her breath away with his gorgeousness!

"I'm very pleased to meet you, Mrs. Chaucer," Ruger said, taking the hand her mother offered to him in greeting.

"How ya doing?" Talli's father asked, striding into the room and offering his own hand to Ruger. "Brent Chaucer."

"Very well, sir, thank you," Ruger responded, giving Brent Chaucer a firm handshake.

Talli's worry that her father would start in to teasing Ruger at any moment began to heighten with every millisecond she and Ruger lingered there with her parents.

Therefore, taking Ruger's hand from her father and clasping it in her own, she said, "Well, there you have it! Ruger, these are my parents. Parents, this is my Ruger, and we better get going."

"No need to hurry off, you two," Alicia said, smiling her warm, motherly smile. "Why don't you sit down and chat with us a while?"

"Not on your life," Talli said, shaking her head and tugging on Ruger's hand as she opened the front door.

"Talli's afraid we'll say or do something weird, Ruger," Brent explained with a chuckle. "Although, now that I think about it, you might be interested in the jar of human teeth I keep on a bookshelf in my office."

"Oh, you're a dentist then, Mr. Chaucer?" Ruger asked as Talli continued to tug on his arm.

"Nope," Brent said, grinning. "I'm an industrial engineer. I just find human teeth very interesting so I—"

"That's enough, Dad. Don't say another word. I'll see you later," Talli said, yanking so hard on Ruger's arm he stumbled toward her a step or two.

"I guess we're leaving then," Ruger chuckled. "It was good to meet you both," he called as Talli "strongly encouraged" him to follow her out of the house. "Have a good evening," he added an instant before Talli closed the door behind them.

Ruger began laughing as he pulled his hand from Talli's grasp, laying his arm across her shoulders. "What? You aren't ready to tell your parents I've decided to marry you?"

Talli sighed with the relief she felt at having escaped with her dad barely having a chance to begin teasing Ruger. "I just didn't want Dad to get started on one of his weird conversation things."

"You mean he doesn't really have a jar full of human teeth in his office?" Ruger asked. He laughed and placed a kiss on her temple.

"Actually, he really does have a jar of human teeth in his office," Talli admitted. "But that's just his way of baiting you so you'll go into his office where he can trap you and...and..."

"Pull my teeth out for his collection?" Ruger teased.

Talli smiled, giggling nervously a moment before exhaling a relieved sigh. "I just didn't want to spend our first night out together with my parents, you know?" she confessed. "Do you think I'm a jerk?"

"Not at all," Ruger assured her. "And I liked the way you called me 'my Ruger,' by the way."

"What?" Talli asked. She'd been in such a hurry to escape the house with Ruger, she wasn't sure what he was referring to.

"You said, 'Ruger, these are my parents...and, parents, this is my Ruger,'" Ruger explained.

Talli gasped. "I did? I'm such an idiot! I'm so sorry. I didn't mean...I mean...I hope you don't think..."

"I think you're awesome," Ruger said. "And I'm hoping that you really do already think of me that way...as yours."

Talli blushed, delighted by his reassurance—delighted by him.

"Now," Ruger said as he opened the passenger door to a big black Dodge pickup. "What do you usually get at Dion's? Pizza? Sub?"

"Mmmm!" Talli moaned. "I'm salivating just thinking about any of it! And I'm good with anything they have...as long as it has green chile on it."

"Me too," he agreed, grinning at her. He reached out and caressed her cheek with the back of his hand. "I'd like to cover you in green chile and..." But he closed the pickup door before he finished his sentence, ensuring Talli couldn't hear what he'd said.

As she watched Ruger slide into the driver's seat, Talli's heart began to swell so much she felt breathless.

"You ready?" he asked, pressing the ignition button and causing the pickup's engine to roar to life.

"Oh, I'm ready," Talli told him. Then, as Ruger pulled away from the curb in front of her house—as she waved to her parents, who were standing at the picture window in the front, watching them drive away—she mumbled to herself, "I've been ready for you since the day I first saw you, Ruger Villarreal."

CHAPTER SEVEN

"We'll have a large Dion's special, Greek salad, and two sides of green chile," Ruger said, placing the order he and Talli had easily agreed on.

"Anything to drink with that, sir?" the young woman serving them asked.

Talli smiled as the girl blushed when Ruger smiled at her and said, "Yeah…a pitcher of water and two large glasses of ice."

Talli understood all too well why the Dion's employee waiting on them was blushing, why she kept giggling inadvertently, and why she now had to ask, "I'm sorry, sir. Did you say a small Dion's special?" Ruger's good looks had befuddled Talli herself for five years, so she'd understood the Frito pie stand girl's reaction to serving Ruger earlier in the day and now this girl's.

"Large," Ruger kindly corrected.

To make matters worse for the cute girl, she didn't look a day over sixteen. And Talli knew that had she herself scorpioned in front of Ruger years before when she'd been only sixteen, she would've dropped dead at his feet rather than talk to him and thank him the way she had that morning.

"And was that the Greek salad you wanted?" the young woman asked, blushing an even deeper blush.

"Yep," Ruger confirmed.

"And I'm so sorry, sir, but what did you say you wanted two sides of?" the girl asked, giggling when Ruger smiled at her with compassion.

"Two sides of green chile," he said. "And a pitcher of water with two large glasses of ice."

The Dion's girl sighed, nodded, and said, "Thank you. I don't know why I'm so rattled today. I'm so sorry, sir."

"It's fine. No worries at all," Ruger reassured her.

Talli, however, knew exactly why the girl was "rattled"—Ruger!

"Thank you. Now the name you want me to put your order under is…" the girl asked.

"Ruger."

"Great! Thanks. And your order should be ready in about twenty minutes, okay?" she nervously informed Ruger.

"Thanks," he said.

"And I'll get the two glasses of ice for you," the order counter girl said. "Do you want water in them, as well? Or just the pitcher of water?"

"You can fill them up now, thanks," Ruger answered.

Talli watched, feeling sorry for the girl as her hands began to tremble as she filled two large glasses with ice and water at the beverage dispenser next to the order counter. At last, she set the two glasses on a tray and offered it to Ruger.

"Here you go," she said, and Talli thought for sure the glasses of ice water would come tumbling off the tray at any moment.

Ruger must've feared the same thing, for he did not pause in reaching out, steadying the tray, and accepting it from the nervous Dion's employee as quickly as possible.

"Thanks," he said again.

"You're very welcome, sir," the nervous teenager giggled.

As he turned, heading for the dining area, Talli looked over her shoulder, winked at the Dion's girl, who was now fanning herself with a paper plate, and mouthed, I know, huh?

"Eee!" the girl exclaimed softly in agreeing response, shaking her head with disbelief at either the fact Ruger was so gorgeous or the fact she'd turned to a mush-brain while taking his order.

"You wanna booth or a table?" Ruger asked.

"Well, if you want me to be entirely honest, I prefer booths myself. But if you'd like a table, that's totally fine with me," she said.

Ruger smiled a brilliant, dazzling, alluring sort of smile and offered, "I prefer booths as well. More privacy, you know?"

"Yeah," Talli said, happy that he was on the same page as she was.

"Is this okay?" Ruger asked, leading her to a booth where they could not only sit in privacy but also have a good view of the order pickup window.

"Perfect," Talli assured him. She thought for a moment of how funny it was that she and Ruger had, in one way or another, been involved in all three meals on the very first day of their official meeting. She'd biffed it at the fiesta grounds, and he'd ended up giving her breakfast—a Villarreal's breakfast burrito. After they'd shared their first kiss—which she still had a hard time wrapping her mind around—they'd enjoyed lunch together on the balloon field. And now, here they were at Dion's for dinner. If she hadn't been living it herself, she wouldn't have believed it.

Balancing the tray with their waters on it in one hand, Ruger set one glass on one side of their table and the other on the opposing side.

"You go ahead and sit down, and I'll get rid of this tray," he explained as he strode toward the front of the restaurant to where the counter for the stacking of used trays was. He grabbed two straws from the dispenser on the utensils counter and turned to head back to where Talli waited.

Talli felt a smile spread across her face as she watched him rather swagger toward her. The thought flitted through Talli's mind that she could sit there in that Dion's booth and just watch him forever! She couldn't keep a quiet giggle of pure pleasure at his handsomeness escape her throat as he sat down across from her.

"I don't know how it can possibly be…but I'm starving," he said in a lowered voice. "You'd think five breakfast burritos and a bowl of Frito pie would've held me over longer."

Talli watched as he tore the paper off his straw, plunged his straw into his glass of ice water, and drank half the glass in no time flat. He handed Talli the other straw he'd retrieved, and she tore open one end of the straw paper.

Ruger watched, smiling as Talli removed the paper sleeve from her straw and then proceeded to peer through the brand-new, freshly unwrapped plastic cylinder before slipping it into her own glass of ice water. An amused chuckle escaped his throat, and she looked up to him, blushing when she realized he'd been watching her.

"Sorry," Talli said, sipping water through the straw.

"For what?" Ruger asked.

"Being a weirdo and looking through my straw before I used it," she answered. "But I've done it for years now…ever since…"

Talli's voice trailed off, and Ruger was certain she was hoping he'd let it go—but he wasn't about to, for now his curiosity was way too piqued.

"For years now, ever since…ever since what?" he prodded.

Again she blushed, and Ruger experienced a thoroughgoing sense of pleasure he'd never known before. Just her smile, her blush, sitting there in a Dion's booth waiting for their pizza caused a huge wave of excitement, of hope, of joy to wash over him.

Talli shook her head, obviously unnerved about the idea of sharing her "ever since" reason for inspecting her straw.

"Come on, baby," Ruger urged with a wink. "You know you can tell me anything."

Talli grinned and, though still blushing, giggled.

"Well, a couple of years ago…" she began. "Okay, so I like to keep a glass of water on my nightstand, right?"

"Who doesn't?" Ruger offered, nodding with encouragement.

"Well, one night I sat up to take a drink of water, and when I did, I felt something in my mouth, right?" she explained.

"Yeah…" Ruger said, stretching the word out in coaxing her to continue.

"I spit the water back into the glass, turned on the lamp on my nightstand, and then began to gag and totally freak out when I saw that it had been a spider I felt in my mouth!" Talli exclaimed, shivering in remembering the horror.

"No way?" Ruger asked, grossed out himself at even the thought.

"Oh yeah!" Talli assured him, shivering again. "It was a disgusting, albeit small, wolf spider…thankfully not those giant-sized ones you see."

Talli seemed to gag a little at the memory, and Ruger withheld his amused chuckle this time—for he could well imagine how awful the experience had been.

"For days and days afterward, I'd nearly throw up every time I thought of it," she admitted.

"Understandably," Ruger offered with sincerity.

"I mean, you read all the urban legends of how every human swallows, like, four to eight spiders a year in their sleep…which, thankfully, is rubbish." She paused, leaned across the table, and added, "I did my research, and it really is rubbish. Although, after nearly drinking a spider myself, it took a lot of research to convince me, you know?"

"I'm sure it did," Ruger responded. "So you use a straw in your glass now so you won't suck up any more spiders?"

But Talli shook her head. "Nope," she answered. "You see, after that totally barfy incident, I bought one of those drink bottles with the built-in straw…you know, so no spider would ever find his way into my open glass again, right?"

"Yeah…"

Talli visibly shivered with disgust once more. "So the very first night that I'm using my new bottle, I woke up, reached over, grabbed it, and took a swig out of the straw. Immediately I felt something other than just water in my mouth, and since the water bottle had a lid on it, I spit the water into my hand and, voilà!"

"No way! Another spider?" Ruger asked, frowning with compassion.

But again Talli shook her head. "Nope. An earwig! A freaking earwig must've been in the straw part because I studied the clear bottle part really well after I washed it. But I left the lid and bottle in the dish drainer, and even though I checked the water in the bottle before I screwed the lid on that night, I did not check the straw. An earwig! A freaking pincher bug earwig thing! Ugh! Again, it was days and days before I stopped feeling like I was going to throw up all the time."

Ruger watched as Talli subconsciously peered through the straw in her glass of ice water before taking another sip.

"So even if it's a brand-new straw, wrapped in paper, you'll check it for earwigs?" Ruger asked. Before she answered, he smiled, nodded, and said, "I can understand that…really."

"Thanks," Talli giggled.

Okay, this girl was too adorable for her own good! Ruger loved listening to her voice—loved hearing the simple yet harrowing story of why she always checked her straws before drinking out of them. Somehow he managed to resist the urge to leap across the table and kiss her like she'd never been kissed before.

Talli took a few long swigs of the refreshing ice water in her glass before commenting, "I do not drink enough water when I'm working the fiesta."

"Me neither," Ruger confirmed. "But when is there time, right?"

"Exactly," Talli agreed. "I mean, it's pretty much go, go, go all morning, you know?"

"I do," Ruger concurred.

Talli watched as Ruger then drank the rest of the water in his glass. She smiled when he drew the rim of the glass to his lips, tipping it so that several pieces of ice tumbled into his mouth.

"So," he began then, crunching on the ice with his molars.

"So what?" Talli asked when he did not continue right away.

"So tell me about this jar of teeth your dad has in his office," he said, smiling. "I mean, if he's not a dentist…"

Talli rolled her eyes and began folding the paper sleeve from her straw back and forth and back and forth to zigzag it like a tiny fan.

"Nope, he's not. But my great-grandfather was," she began. "He was a dentist, like, way back in the day, you know…like, a hundred years ago. And whenever he had to pull someone's tooth or teeth, he cleaned them up and plopped them in a jar."

"The teeth, not the people, right?" Ruger teased.

Talli smiled. "Yeah…the teeth, not the people."

"And…" Ruger prodded.

"And…he had jars and jars and jars of teeth by the time he retired," Talli explained. "I guess he was really intrigued with human teeth, you know? Anyway, when he passed away, my great-grandmother gave every grandchild a huge glass jar full of human teeth. She said it's what my great-grandpa had meant to do for years and had just never gotten around to it. Although my dad says he thinks his grandpa just never wanted to give them up. I guess it was pretty normal to walk into Great-Grandpa's office and find him sorting teeth all over the top of his desk and studying them with a magnifying glass."

"Wow," Ruger said, handsome eyebrows arched. "Cool hobby."

Talli laughed and shook her head. "Oh, but it gets better," she told him.

"How could it get any better?" Ruger asked, smiling.

"Well, apparently Great-Grandpa Chaucer had his favorites," she answered.

"You mean…his favorite grandchildren?"

"No…his favorite pulled teeth," Talli confessed. "And Great-Grandma gave one to each of us great-grandchildren. I'll admit, mine is pretty awesome."

Ruger could not keep the smile already on his face from spreading wider and wider. The longer he was in Talli's company, the more interesting he found her to be.

"Oh? What's so awesome about the one you have?" he asked, nearly desperate to keep her talking about her great-grandfather's odd hobby.

He laughed a little in his throat when Talli's eyes widened with excitement as she began, "Well, I kind of like to think of mine as something to really be treasured. It's a canine tooth that a man from Ireland had had capped with gold when he was a young man. But when he immigrated to the United States in, like, the 1930s, he found himself in need of money. So he begged my great-grandfather to pull it for him so he could salvage the gold and sell it to feed his family. Of course, normally my great-grandfather wouldn't agree to such a thing as wasting a tooth. When he examined the man, it was clear the tooth was very loose and would eventually fall out on its own. Still, the old Irishman was desperate, and so my grandfather pulled it for him. But instead of giving it to the man, he bought it from him…paying him more than the little bit of gold would've been worth even back then because…well, because…"

"Because he was a nice guy?" Ruger offered. Then before Talli could answer, he added, "And because he wanted it for his collection, right?"

Talli laughed, and her pretty cheeks pinked up with mild embarrassment. Nodding, she admitted, "Yep. My great-grandfather did have a kind heart, so I'm sure that was the biggest reason he bought the old Irishman's tooth. Still, I'm fairly certain his wanting it for his collection played a big part in it, as well."

Ruger chuckled, leaned back in his seat, and said, "That is a pretty awesome story. No wonder you love your tooth."

Again Talli laughed. "Yep, I actually do. In fact, when my great-grandmother gave it to me…well, before she gave it to me, she had it encased in a gold and glass locket."

"And do you wear it?" Ruger inquired with interest. "Like maybe at Halloween time with your Dracula Sucks sweatshirt?"

Shaking her head as she continued to laugh, Talli managed, "No…no. Not on Halloween. But if you want to know the truth, I do kind of love it, and I will wear it on a long chain with a sweater now and then in the fall and winter." She shrugged, adding, "I mean, believe it or not, it's a great conversation piece."

"Oh, I'm sure it is!" Ruger exclaimed. "I'm sure it is."

Talli felt a little sick to her stomach with sudden worrisome anxiety. After all, she was on a date with the man of her dreams—a dinner date, which meant they were both thinking of food—and she'd already told him two of the grossest things about herself that existed! Nearly drinking live spiders and earwigs? Human teeth? Both very unappetizing topics of conversation! What had she been thinking?

The truth was, she hadn't been thinking! Not at all! She'd felt so instantaneously comfortable in Ruger's company that she'd just rattled off in-depth answers to the two simple questions he'd asked.

Horrified, Talli nervously blurted, "So? Did you sell any more chainsaw sculptures today? Not that I'm being nosey or anything. I'm just thinking you might want to discuss something besides bugs and dead people's teeth before our food is ready."

Talli relaxed a little when Ruger folded his muscular forearms on the table, leaned toward her, and answered, "I did. In fact—and I don't ever share this kind of information with anyone—but I made fifty grand today at the fiesta."

Talli closed her mouth once she'd realized it had fallen agape in astonishment.

"Fifty grand? In one day?" she asked in a whisper. "That's more than I make in year! Like…a lot more!"

"Maybe," Ruger said, shrugging, however. "But you provide a service to people, and I just hack away at logs and stuff."

Talli smiled, "Oh, don't try to downplay your success. I think it's awesome! I mean, art…it's a gift you have to be born with, you know? It's one of those things that amaze me, how people can use paint or pencils—or chainsaws—and make these beautiful images and sculptures." Talli shook her head with awe. "You're gifted, and I'm glad you're able to make a living with your art."

Ruger grinned, reached across the table, and covered Talli's hand where it lay with his own.

"Wow, that was a nice thing to say," he said. "I get told quite often that I should quit the chainsaw carving thing and get a real job. So it's nice to hear something supportive for a change."

Talli frowned, trying to remain calm. "People who say things like that, they're just envious," she told him. She shook her head with disgust. "If you think about it, it's always the wannabes that criticize the accomplishments of others. I hope you don't take any of it to heart, because it's just envy. They're just jealous."

Ruger's handsome brow pulled together in a frown. "Sounds to me like you've had some experience of your own along that line, hmmm?"

Talli shrugged again. "Who doesn't, you know? At one time or another, everyone is the victim of poopy people being jerks."

Ruger's smile returned, and he nodded. "Well said. At one time or another, everyone is the victim of poopy people being jerks…though you used kinder language than I would have to say the same thing."

Talli blushed, feeling like a dork for actually using the phrase poopy people.

"So I was wondering," Ruger began then, "do you meet a lot of poopy people in your line of work? I mean, the only person that I know—well, that I know personally—who gets, like, facial treatments and stuff is my sister Kimber. And she's kind of a…well, she can be…you know, a poopy person sometimes. You know, real bossy and picky about stuff, kind of thinking she knows more than the person who really knows. So is everyone you work on like that? Or what?"

Talli smiled, shaking her head, "No, not at all! And I'm really glad because I couldn't do what I do if everyone was a jerk, you know? Nope…most of my clients are awesome!" She paused, winking at Ruger as she added, "I mean, they feel relaxed and pampered when they're in my care…so they treat me really well."

"Good," Ruger stated. "They should." Ruger grinned an alluring, mischievous grin, lowered his voice, and said, "I know I'd feel relaxed and pampered in your care."

Talli blushed and bit her lip with delight at his flirting. "Oh, and I'd make sure that you did," she responded in a near whisper.

Ruger smiled, thoroughly pleased by her flirting with him in response to his flirting with her. He felt goose bumps at the back of his neck—wished he'd gotten their Dion's order to go so he could whisk Talli Chaucer away to privacy of his house and…

"People are going to think we're stupid, you know," he said, attempting to redirect his thoughts where Talli was concerned.

"I'm sure they will," she said, her smile fading.

"Are you up for it?" Ruger asked, concerned about what her answer might be. He knew she felt as he did—knew she was as serious about him as he was about her. Still, when the idiot know-it-alls of the world started bombarding them with warnings and criticism—which Ruger knew they would—he needed reassurance that she was as tough as he thought she was in standing up for herself.

"Oh yeah," Talli said firmly. "I'm a big girl, and I can take it. It's like my brothers always say…"

"And what's that?" Ruger asked. "What do your brothers always say? And while we're at it…how many overprotective brothers do I have to look forward to meeting?"

Talli smiled. "Two. And…uh…they're both cops…just so you're prepared."

"Nice," Ruger chuckled. "Cops. That's not intimidating at all."

"Oh, don't worry," Talli assured him. "They're the kind of cops everyone likes—bad to the bone as far as defensive tactics and gun competitions…but the nicest, most caring guys I've ever known." She paused, blushed a little, and added, "Until I met you this morning and you gave me your cook's apron for my scraped-up chin."

Ruger smiled, figuring she'd only just remembered the cute little scrape on her chin, being that she quickly rested her chin on one hand to hide it.

"That's good to know," he said. "But you never did tell me what it is your brothers always say."

"Oh yeah," Talli said, smiling. "When it comes to other people's opinions and drama, the boys always quote some movie they liked as kids. They say, 'Screw you, guys! I hate high school!'"

Ruger laughed. "Meaning unwanted opinions and drama are so immature and insignificant…so high school, right? I liked that movie too."

"Yep," Talli affirmed. "That's what my brothers always taught me to think—actually, to even say sometimes—when people get in my business. So you don't have to worry about me. I can take it."

Talli frowned when Ruger's laughter and happy countenance instantly turned to a frown as he looked past her to something beyond for a moment.

"Well, I hope you're feeling tough right now," he grumbled, "because it looks like we're about to have our first round of sh…crap."

Talli turned in her seat to look over her shoulder. Coming toward them was a drop-dead gorgeous, dark-haired young woman. Her attention was riveted on Ruger, and as she approached, a rather fake-looking smile spread across her face as she exclaimed, "Ruger! What are you doing here?"

Talli's heart sank—for in truth, she did not feel prepared or confident enough to face an old girlfriend of his. Especially one that looked like she'd just stepped off the Miss Universe stage.

"Hey, Kimber," Ruger said, again nearly growling. "The question is what are you doing here?"

"I saw your truck in the parking lot as I was driving by," the beauty answered. "So I thought I'd whip around and see if you were up to having dinner with me." The beautiful woman slid into the booth bench next to Ruger. "But I see you already have company," she said, smiling her fake smile at Talli.

"Yep. I do," Ruger said bluntly.

"Well? Aren't you going to introduce me?" the woman asked.

Exhaling a heavy sigh, Ruger released Talli's hand, slumped back against the booth bench, and said, "Talli, this is Kimber...my nosey, intrusive sister."

CHAPTER EIGHT

"It's nice to meet you, Talli," Ruger's sister said, tucking a strand of long black hair behind one perfect ear.

"You too," Talli managed to respond, forcing her own fake smile.

In truth, she didn't know whether to burst into tears of relief because the gorgeous woman was Ruger's sister and not an old girlfriend—or jump up and run in feeling so thoroughly plain and dowdy in her company. She figured it made sense that, like Colt, the other members of Ruger's family would be gorgeous, considering how gorgeous Ruger was. Still, it was a hard pill to swallow—sitting at the same table with a woman who owned any room she walked into the way Kimber obviously would.

"We're busy, Kimber," Ruger stated somewhat rudely to his sister.

Kimber smiled and tossed her head, sending a curtain of glorious raven hair cascading down her back. "Oh, come on, bro. I'm your sister! I'm sure you ordered enough for me too," she said.

"Nope. I didn't," Ruger answered. "And this is a date—one I've been looking forward to longer than you know. So you've said hello…and now you can leave."

Talli felt her eyes widen a bit; she was pretty astonished at Ruger's blunt, kind of ill-mannered behavior. It seemed uncharacteristic for him. Even though she'd only known him a short time, his curtness with his sister really did not seem warranted. Still, though Talli's heart and soul recognized Ruger as the man she'd always dreamt of finding, she did not recognize his sister in any regard. Ruger knew his sister; Talli did not. And after all, hadn't he just finished telling her that his sister could be one of those "poopy people"?

"Eee!" Kimber Albuquerque–sing-sang. Smiling and dramatically arching her perfectly shaped eyebrows feigning offense, Kimber winked at Talli and added, "He must really want to get you alone, huh?"

"Well, I hope so," Talli said, forcing a smile. "But it was really nice to meet you."

Ruger smiled at Talli, nodding in approval. She could tell he liked that she hadn't tried to defend Kimber—or convince Ruger to let her stay. In truth, Talli's nature dictated that she normally would've done just that—tried to smooth things over between Ruger and Kimber by fibbing and saying she wouldn't mind if Kimber joined them. But the truth was, Ruger was too important to her; their date was too important to her. Talli and Ruger had both implied and confessed some pretty heavy stuff to one another during that first day of the balloon fiesta, and Talli wasn't about to endanger their novice relationship for anything—not even the feelings of a family member. And that very fact, in and of itself, was further evidence to Talli of how desperately she wanted Ruger for herself!

"Well, good for you, Sally," Kimber said with a firm nod. "I can see you're not going to let anything mess up your chance at my brother, hmmm."

"It's Talli, Kimber, and you know it," Ruger grumbled. "And it's me that's not going to let anything mess up my chance with her. So we'll see you another time, okay?"

Talli exhaled the breath she'd been holding as she realized Ruger's temperament was softening.

"You mean you're not going to let me stay? Even for a minute?" Kimber pressed, however.

The beautiful young woman pouted her lower lip, and Talli was sure that Ruger's sister was pretty used to getting whatever she wanted by doing so—at least with men who were not her brother.

"Nope," Ruger said.

Talli's eyes widened again as she watched Ruger take hold of his sister's arm, rather push her out of the seat, and stand with her.

"But I'll walk you out to your car, Nineteen-Eleven," he said, forcing a smile, "just to make sure you make it safe and sound."

"He's determined, isn't he?" Kimber asked Talli. The beauty's smile faded, however, as she mumbled, "I guess we'll get to know each other better another time, Talli."

"I guess so," Talli said, trying to sound as kind as possible.

"I'll be right back," Ruger said over his shoulder as he rather marched Kimber toward the exit.

Talli couldn't help but smile and giggle a little, thinking that both her cop brothers would wholeheartedly approve of the way Ruger was marching "a problem" out of the door.

Talli took a long drink of ice water through her earwig-free straw and tried to settle her nerves. It was a sure thing that Kimber wasn't going to be a Talli fan—not with the way Talli had supported Ruger in his endeavors to preserve their privacy. Yet she figured Colt didn't have any problems with her. And if she continued to slather him with free funnel cakes during the week, Talli figured she'd at least have Ruger's brother on her side.

Her hands were trembling, and she linked them for a moment to try and steady them. Kimber didn't seem like the kind of woman anyone wanted to make an enemy of. But Ruger had championed Talli through the entire, albeit short, incident. Therefore, Talli reminded herself that it wasn't Kimber she was hoping to marry: it was Ruger.

"There," Talli whispered aloud to herself. "I've just admitted it again. I want to marry him."

Peering through her straw first—even though she knew it was arachnid- as well as insect-free—Talli sucked up another big gulp of ice water.

"Don't freak out, Talli," she whispered to herself. "Most people have at least one difficult family member, right? Just don't freak out. Remain calm, and don't freak out."

"Man, you're lucky I love you, Kimber," Ruger growled as he opened the driver's side door to Kimber's red Challenger for her.

"Oh, don't be all mad, Ruger," Kimber pouted. "I had to get a look at your new little thing, didn't I?"

Ruger gritted his teeth to keep from saying something he might later regret while reprimanding his sister for interfering in his evening with Talli.

"She's not my new little thing, Kimber," he growled. "I've had my eye on Talli for years, and today…today I finally got my shot at her. So don't even start trying to play your head games with me in this situation."

Kimber frowned as she slid into the driver's seat of her car.

"Look, Ruger," she began, "I know you've got this 'saving myself for marriage' thing going, okay? And I respect that."

"No, you don't," Ruger stated, still holding his tongue from saying what his temper really wanted to let go at Kimber.

"Whatever, baby brother," Kimber said, rolling her eyes with mild intolerance. "But I just think...well, to be honest, your nerd thing of waiting until you're married to have sex...waiting until you find the one girl just right for you and marry her, expecting to live all happily ever after? Well, you're tired of it, and this girl just presented herself as the easiest prey for you to wrap around your little finger, doing whatever you say because she's so smitten by your good looks. She's easy to snap up, and you're ready to be finished with your life of, quote, 'saving yourself.'" Kimber shook her head, adding, "You sound like some girl that's gone to a Christian mingle and promised her guitar-toting, folk-song-singing, handsome young pastor that she'll keep herself pure until—"

As all the anger and frustration he was feeling toward his sister reach its zenith, Ruger slammed the driver's side door of his sister's car, startling her into silence inside.

"Good night, Kimber," Ruger told her through the window. "And please...don't push me to the point that I have to choose between my relationship with you and my relationship with Talli."

"What relationship?" Kimber screamed from within her car. "You've known the chick one day, Ruger!"

"Good night, Kimber," Ruger said once more before turning and heading back toward the Dion's entrance.

Ruger shook his head as he heard the engine of Kimber's Challenger roar to life—gritted his teeth when he heard tires squeal as she hauled butt out of the parking lot.

It took him a good thirty seconds to convince himself that he loved his sister—didn't really hate her—even for all his frustration. It seemed every family had one kid that the other kids whispered about from time to time—one kid whose personality was so polar opposite of everyone else's and caused everyone to silently wonder whether he or she were the milkman's child or something. Kimber was that kid in Ruger's family. Ruger, three brothers, and two sisters—six children had been born to Alejandro and Hailey Villarreal. Five Villarreal kids were pretty much exactly alike in their way of thinking, their goals, their ambitions and opinions of what constituted a healthy relationship. Colt, Barret, Browning, Ruger, and their sister Beretta got along well and enjoyed spending time together and having meaningful or lighthearted conversation. Kimber, however, was the cliché black sheep of the family, and no matter how patient everyone else in the family was with her, eventually somebody lost their cool. Every one of Ruger's siblings had endured at least one episode of being estranged from Kimber at some point. And even though Ruger had avoided the necessity of not speaking with his sister for an extended amount of time in order to keep his cool, he knew that Talli could and probably very well would be the thing that might cause him to cut Kimber out of his life—at least for a period of time.

Sure, he'd avoid it coming to that, if possible. But as he stepped into Dion's and strode toward the booth where Talli sat looking a little pale, and peering through the straw in her glass of water, he knew that he would never let Kimber upset Talli again. Even if it meant he never spoke to his sister for the rest of his life!

"Sorry about that," Ruger said as he slid onto the booth bench next to Talli. Talli grinned, delighted that he had chosen to slide in next to her, rather than sit on the bench across the table from her.

She liked the comforting sensation of his warm body against hers as he put one strong arm around her shoulders and tucked her securely under his arm.

"You might as well know that Nineteen-Eleven can be a bi— A-a..." he began, stammering in trying to think of another word that could describe his sister's aggravating behavior.

"A beeotch?" Talli finished, smiling.

Ruger smiled as well, brushed a strand of hair from her cheek, and answered, "Well, that's putting it mildly. But since I'm not sure how you feel about, you know...stronger language..."

Talli giggled, admitting, "Oh, you could've said what you were going to say. I could just tell you didn't want to."

Warmth akin to sitting through a Phoenix sunset washed over Talli then as Ruger pressed a long, lingering kiss to her temple.

"Thanks," he said. "That's good to know. And I should explain why our family calls her Nineteen-Eleven, I suppose."

"I'm guessing because she's named after the Kimber 1911 pistol," Talli offered.

When Ruger's handsome brows arched with approving astonishment, Talli looked up to him, saying, "Dude, both of my brothers are cops. Do you think two cops would let their little sister linger in ignorance when it comes to firearms?"

Ruger laughed. "No, I suppose not."

"And it's okay," Talli continued. "Kimber, I mean. I'm sure she's just protective of you."

"Well, that's a little true, I suppose," Ruger halfheartedly agreed. "But I think the real reason is she's a little too much of a stuck-up bi...beeotch, control freak. She doesn't like the fact that she didn't choose you for me."

Talli's own brows arched then. "Are you saying that she has chosen for you in the past?"

"She's tried…and crashed and burned," Ruger confirmed. "But please don't let her showing up here bother you at all, okay? Or her snarky personality. She's just hard to deal with sometimes…most of the time, actually."

"It's all right," Talli rather fibbed. After all, she was very bothered, not so much by Kimber's crashing their date for a few minutes but because Kimber didn't think Talli was of a high enough caliber for Ruger. Talli herself had her doubts, but their mutual and instant magnetism to one another, the fact that he had told her his feelings almost right off the bat—well, Talli wanted to exert some self-confidence. She knew she would never be good enough for Ruger in Kimber's eyes; she'd just have to focus on Ruger and not his beeotch of a sister.

"Ruger? Your order is ready," came a voice over the Dion's intercom system.

Ruger slid off the bench, standing. Wagging a finger at Talli, he said, "Now, you stay right here. Don't move a muscle. I'll be right back."

"Okay," Talli agreed.

She watched him saunter toward the order pickup counter. Dang, he looked good in those jeans! Talli grinned as every other woman in the restaurant seemed to be thinking the same thing. One might think "popped-out eyeball soup" would need to be added to the Dion's menu with the way the women were gawking at him.

From where she sat, Talli could see Ruger approach the order pickup window. The same young woman who had totally lost her composure while taking their order from Ruger was now handing him a pizza and a bowl of salad. The girl blushed redder than Santa's suit as Ruger thanked her and turned to head back toward the booth.

"And dinner is served," Ruger announced, spinning the pizza pan as he slid it onto the table. "Here's the salad. I'll get some plates and forks."

"Thanks," Talli said, accepting the covered bowl of salad with two small plastic containers of green chile and two plastic containers of Dion's famous Greek salad dressing balanced on top of it.

Ruger did indeed hurry in retrieving some paper plates and forks, returning in just a few seconds.

"Mmmm!" he moaned as he sat down across the table from Talli. "Are you starving or what?"

"I am!" Talli admitted.

"Here. How much do you want?" Ruger asked, taking the lid off the delicious Dion's Greek salad and using the plastic salad spoons he'd retrieved to grasp a nice amount of the good stuff.

"Oh, you can pile it on!" Talli answered. "I love their salad. They don't skip the feta cheese, you know?"

"I know, huh?" Ruger said, plopping a mountain of salad onto one of the paper plates. "There you go."

"Thanks." Talli watched as Ruger loaded another paper plate with salad and then pushed the salad bowl and spoons to one side.

"Best salad in town," he mumbled, taking one of the small plastic containers of Dion's Greek dressing and pulling back the foil tab to open it.

"Oh, it so is," Talli agreed. "My dad has a friend in Arizona, and every time he goes down there to, like, watch a football or basketball game with him, Dad takes some Dion's dressing to him in a cooler."

"Well, I'd sure miss it if I couldn't have it readily available." Ruger paused, spearing a large piece of feta cheese on his plastic fork. "I mean, look at this one! It's huge...and I love the huge ones."

Talli giggled as Ruger put the piece of feta cheese in his mouth, closed his eyes, and moaned, "Mmmmm! I was so hungry." He ate a couple of bites of salad in silence then. "I probably wouldn't have been as impatient with Kimber if I hadn't been so hungry, you know?"

"Oh, are you one of those men?" Talli asked, smiling. "One of those guys who gets hangry when he needs to eat?"

Ruger shrugged his broad shoulders. "Not really. Just a little impatient with some things, I guess. And Kimber can tick me off on a full stomach whether or not I'm hungry, so I guess I didn't do too bad."

"I thought you handled it very well," Talli offered.

Again Ruger shrugged and took a few more bites of salad before responding, "I don't know. I try to be patient with her, but she's so, you know, irritating. Mom and Dad keep telling her that if she doesn't learn to be less self-centered, she's never gonna find a man to put up with her."

"Well, she's so beautiful I'm sure most men would be willing to overlook a couple of mild...um...character flaws," Talli said.

"Oh, believe me, they do not see anything wrong with her at all. Not at first," Ruger admitted. "Until about a month or so in, and then...you know how in those old cartoons the roadrunner takes off from the coyote and leaves a cloud of dust? That's a guy's reaction once he really gets to know Kimber."

Talli smiled, amused at his analogy—even though she knew she shouldn't be.

"Anyway, no more talking about my sister," Ruger sighed. "It'll give me a stomachache."

A quiet giggle escaped Talli's throat. Poor Ruger—having a sister that stressed him out the way Kimber did. She was glad she and her brothers got along so well. She couldn't imagine not having good relationships with them—not ever.

"Okay, so what do you want to talk about?" Talli began. "The food? The balloon fiesta? The weather?"

"Us," Ruger said without pause. "Let's talk about us."

Talli blushed and felt a thrill travel down her spine—butterflies erupt in her stomach. He was already referring to them as an "us"? She was over the moon with being pleased!

"Us?" she prodded.

"Yep, us," he confirmed. "Now, this thing with my sister tonight, it shows that, you and me, we're gonna have to be confident in ourselves, in us being an us...and to hell with everyone else, you know?"

Talli's smile broadened. She liked his matter-of-fact manner—his seeming lack of doubt in them being an "us."

"I mean, Kimber will probably be the hardest to deal with," he began. He reached out and took a piece of pizza from the large pan in the center of the table between them. He plopped it on the paper plate now void of any evidence a salad had ever been there, save some soft swirls of lingering salad dressing.

"My brothers and my other sister will be all good. They know me well enough to know I'm not a player or stupid," he said. "What about your family? Think any of them will give us any trouble for jumping in so fast?"

Talli shook her head. "Not really," she said. "My brothers probably already have you checked out by now. I'm sure Dad called them the minute we left."

"Good for them. They sound like a couple of good guys," Ruger said, grinning at her and causing goose bumps to return to her arms and legs. "I don't have a criminal record or anything, so hopefully they'll see that as a plus."

"Oh, definitely," Talli laughed. "And like you said, my family knows I'm smart too…that my instincts are good. If they are worried, they'll sit back and let things unfold…let me decide for myself."

"Okay, good," he mumbled, taking a bite of his pizza.

Talli reached out and chose a smaller piece of pizza, taking a bite before placing it on her plate. At once the delicious blend of pizza crust and sauce, mingled with Italian sausage, smoked ham, pepperoni, mushrooms, black olives, red onions, and of course green chile, caused Talli to breathe a satisfied, "Mmmm!" herself. Talli couldn't imagine there was another pizza in all the world that tasted any better than a Dion's Special. Of course, she knew that it was the green chile on the special that made most New Mexicans fall in love with it. She figured everyone in every state everywhere had their own favorite hometown pizza—loved theirs like no other. Still, without green chile as a topping, she had a hard time imagining any pizza anywhere could ever really come close.

She watched as Ruger used his plastic fork to scoop some green chile out of his side container and spread it on his piece of pizza.

"So, I'm also thinking…I mean, I hope I'm not being too presumptuous," he began. "But do you want us to hold off on the physical affection for a while? I mean, I don't want you to think I'm only after you because of your body, you know?"

Talli choked a little—astonished at his forthrightness.

"I mean, because you so have a great body," he continued, winking at her. "You're gorgeous all the way around, and I do want to—you know—have a physical relationship with you…you know, proper physical relationship with you. But I don't want you to think that's all I'm about. So? Do you want to hold off on me kissing you anymore for a while, or what?"

He offered a chin-thrust of encouraging her to answer him and then took another bite of his pizza, which was now heaping with green chile.

"Well, you sure don't mess around, do you?" Talli giggled.

"Not where you're concerned," Ruger stated. "I don't want to do anything to make you uncomfortable and risk messing us up. So just be honest with me…hands off?"

Talli blushed and glanced down as she used her fork to ladle some green chile out of her little plastic side cup. "Where's the fun in that?" she asked flirtatiously.

"Damn, girl!" Ruger exclaimed under his breath. "Are you sure we just met for the first time today? Because I could swear you know me better than anybody else does already."

Talli said, "I'm sure," before taking a swig of ice water. She loved her green chile, but the green chile at Dion's had a good bite to it tonight.

"I mean, don't misunderstand me," Ruger began, his dark brows puckering with sudden concern. "I'm not a…I mean…I'm not asking about anything beyond…you know…"

"Making out?" Talli finished for him.

"Yeah!" he chuckled. "I'm kind of prude about, you know…people having…you know…people…"

"Being sexually active before they're married?" Talli finished for him again.

"Exactly!" he again chuckled with obvious relief.

Talli couldn't believe how quickly she was becoming so comfortable with Ruger. She'd never had a conversation about physical boundaries with a guy she'd dated before—let alone a conversation about it that didn't make her edgy.

"What's your take on it?" he asked.

He was still frowning, and Talli knew then that he had shown his hand to her on the subject first on purpose—as to make her more comfortable in revealing hers.

"Same as yours," she answered without any reservation.

"Sweet," he said as his frown disappeared and a smile stole across his alluring mouth once more. "And now that that's out of the way," he continued, "tell me about yourself…something besides the fact that you work the funnel cake stand at the fiesta every year and that you relax people's faces and make their skin better."

"Okay," Talli agreed, wiping her fingers on the napkin in her lap. "But only if you go back and forth with me—you know, swap information."

"You got it," he agreed. "Go on. You first," he urged with a nod as he took another piece of pizza.

As Talli's brain scrambled for something interesting to tell about herself—something a man the likes of Ruger Villarreal would find interesting—she still couldn't believe that a mere fourteen hours before, she'd simply been excited to set eyes on the sexy burrito guy who worked the breakfast burrito stand at the balloon fiesta for one week out of the year. Yet now here she sat—sitting across from him at Dion's with the wonderful sensation of the green chile burn on her lips and tongue, knowing that his lips and tongue were feeling the same way, and anticipating that they might share that delicious burn as their mouths met later that night when he dropped her at home. But it was the consciousness of the green chile burn itself that was proof it was all really happening—that she wasn't just dreaming— that she really was on a date with Ruger Villarreal!

♥

"Well, here we are," Talli nervously stated as she ascended the last step to the front porch.

"We certainly are here," Ruger said, stepping up to stand before her.

She didn't know why, but on the ride home from Dion's, Talli had begun to grow nervous—anxious even. She surmised it was probably because she'd been up way before dawn for the balloon fiesta, met and fell in love with the man of her dreams, and enjoyed a heavy meal of Greek salad and pizza with green chile at Dion's—all in a matter of a mere seventeen hours. It was enough to make anyone tired and weak-minded.

"I don't about you, but I'm worn out," Ruger said as he reached out, gathering Talli into his arms and against the warm strength of his body.

"Me too," Talli sighed, snuggling against him. She slipped her arms around his waist, returning his embrace and feeling instantly comforted. He liked her! He really, really liked her. It wasn't an act— a farce—she could tell by the way he held her, slowly swaying back and forth a just a tiny bit. Whether the swaying was intentional or just a consequence of fatigue, Talli found it incredibly soothing.

"So, five thirty in the morning?" Ruger asked. "I think that's plenty early, since we don't really care about the dawn patrol tomorrow."

"Perfect," Talli assured him.

Ruger looked down, and Talli looked up to find him gazing at her, his eyes narrowed and an expression of contentment on his gorgeous face.

"It'll be fun," he commented, "me and you at the fiesta watching the balloons and snapping cameras like a couple of tourists. I figure we'll start with a breakfast burrito—"

"And hot chocolate," Talli added.

"Of course," he agreed. "A breakfast burrito and hot chocolate before the balloons go up and a couple of fresh funnel cakes once they're aloft and gone, hmmm?"

"Perfect," Talli giggled.

He ended his embrace of her as his hands moved to cup her face. Talli thought she might simply "swoon away," as her grandmother used to say, as Ruger continued to gaze down at her. His eyes were piercing, even for the fact they looked almost black there in the dark on her parents' front porch.

"Don't doubt me, Talli," he said in a lowered, fascinating voice that was provocative to the point of weakening her knees. "When it's late like it is now, and we're tired—when we're apart—don't doubt me. Don't doubt us. I've never had an experience like this in my life, this feeling of certainty…of instantly knowing what should be, what will be. I know you had the same perception today and that it seems surreal…impossible. But it's not. We're meant for each other, and we both know it, so don't doubt. Text me, call me…any time day or night, okay? If you're worried or doubting, I promise, I'll come running to you with reassurance. I'll come running to you…or you can run to me. Okay? No matter what."

Talli smiled as an old song her grandmother used to sing when Talli was little began playing in her mind.

"What?" Ruger asked, grinning. "Did I say something funny? Or are you just glad to know you've got me where you want me?"

Talli smiled as her heart swelled with an incredible joy she'd never known before. "I...I'm in awe that this is all happening. And...well, an old song my grandma used to sing when I was little just popped into my head when you said I could run to you."

"What song?" Ruger asked, his eyes narrowing even more.

"It's silly," Talli mumbled.

"Tell me," he prodded, smiling.

"Well, I'm sure you've never heard of it. It was, like, from the '70s or something...by this old band called the Bee Gees," she began to explain.

She gasped, however, when Ruger laughed a little and then gathered her into his arms again as he began to sway again and sang, "Run to me whenever you're lonely. Run to me if you need a shoulder..."

"Now and then, you need someone older," Talli interjected.

"So darlin', you run to me," Ruger sang with her.

As they both burst into laughter, Talli shook her head with disbelief.

"You know that song?" she asked through her giggles of delight. "You know who the Bee Gees are?"

"Of course!" Ruger assured her. "My grandma is a huge Bee Gees fan! She really loves Barry Gibb. And I mean, why not? That bro had way badass hair."

Talli laughed as Ruger began to sway with her again and, in an incredibly sexy, low voice that sounded nothing like the Bee Gees, sang, "Run to me whenever you're lonely. Run to me if you need a shoulder. Now and then when you want to smolder...then, darlin', you run to me."

"When I want to smolder?" Talli giggled.

"Oh yes, querida," he mumbled as his head descended toward hers. "Smolder."

Ruger didn't fiddle around any longer but took Talli's face between his warm, strong hands once more and kissed her.

Talli could feel his breath on her cheek as his lips tenderly toyed with hers at first, offering soft, slow kisses that seemed to be meant to coax her reassuringly, drawing her to him—against him—until he sensed she was comfortable with a more passionate exchange between them. In mere moments more, Talli felt her hands slip around his waist—move up his muscular back to grasp his shoulders in trying to somehow be closer to him.

Kissing Ruger Villarreal was like existing in a dream! Talli felt as if there were no weight to her body, as if she were floating on the proverbial cloud. All there was to her in those moments was the mad pounding of her heart as Ruger's mouth rained euphoria over her—as the warm moisture of his kiss imprinted on her mind and senses that there would never be anything more physically irresistible and magnificent than kissing him!

And he was profoundly gifted at kissing—one moment teasing her with soft, playful, coaxing kisses and the next grinding his mouth to hers with such demanding passion that it nearly took her breath from her to reciprocate it!

All too soon, Ruger's mouth left Talli's, coming to rest at her neck just under her left ear.

"Thanks for not putting the 'keep your hands off me' stipulation on me, Talli," he whispered into her ear.

"Thank you for not putting that stipulation on me," she whispered in return, and goose bumps rippled over every inch of her body as he slowly exhaled a warm breath on her neck.

Ruger pressed a soft kiss to her lips, inhaling a deep breath and exhaling a sigh as he said, "So good night, and I'll see you in the morning."

"Good night," Talli managed, wildly disappointed when he released her.

"And remember," he added, gazing down at her, "If you start to worry...or doubt..."

"Run to you," Talli finished.

"That's right," Ruger affirmed.

He winked at her, kissed her quickly on the forehead, and then turned and sauntered down the front porch steps.

Talli watched him walking toward his truck, suddenly becoming more and more aware of the cool of the evening the farther he strode away from her.

All at once, he paused, turned, and looked back at her. "Hey, did we just find our song already or what?" he asked.

"We did!" Talli giggled.

Tossing a chin-thrust of approval at her, Ruger called, "See you at five thirty, my little Bee Gee."

"Okay," Talli called before opening the front door and stepping into the house.

Quickly she went to the front room window, watching as Ruger got into his pickup. He waved as he pulled away from the curb, and smiling with delight, Talli waved back.

She couldn't walk to her bedroom—not yet. Her legs were still too weak from the effects of Ruger's kiss. Plopping down on the sofa, she was surprised when she felt her phone vibrate. Reaching into her back pocket, she retrieved it, smiling as she saw a text from Ruger.

No doubts, no worries, baby. Just run to me if you need me. Text me if you're too tired to run. There was a wink face emoji at the end of the text.

Talli exhaled a sigh of not only fatigue but also wonder and joy. The sexy burrito guy she'd been dreaming about for five years—and not just during the balloon fiesta but all year long for five long years—was going to be hers! She was going to belong to him!

Closing her eyes for a little while, Talli rested her head on the back of the sofa, savored the lingering sensation of the whisker burn Ruger's face had caused on the tender flesh around her lips, and quietly sang, "Am I unwise to open up your eyes, to love me. Run to me whenever you're lonely. Run to me if you need a shoulder. Now and then you need someone older. So, darlin', you run to me."

Smiling, a quiet giggle bubbled in her throat. "Now and then when you want to smolder…then, darlin', you run to me," she sang in a whisper.

CHAPTER NINE

The following morning proved to be more incredible than any balloon fiesta mass ascension that Talli had ever witnessed—not because of more than eight hundred multihued hot air balloons that launched in wave after vivid wave to generate a kaleidoscope of color across the azure background of Albuquerque's sky (although that, in itself, was awe-inspiring) but because Talli had experienced the wonder with Ruger! Every aspect of the fiesta seemed more glorious, more beautiful, more breathtaking than ever before in Ruger's company. The air seemed fresher, the food seemed more delicious, the flames of the balloon burners seemed brighter. Everything was escalated to a higher degree when Ruger was with her!

As he had so aptly predicted the night before, both Ruger and Talli looked like a couple of out-of-state tourists as the shutters on their cameras clicked away, so often in unison, as they each attempted to capture the sights, sounds, and very essence of the most colorful show on earth. Ruger and Talli ate breakfast burritos, drank hot chocolate, talked to balloon pilots, munched on funnel cake, and watched balloons rise into the air as they stood wrapped in each other's arms.

The entire day was like something out of a dream! Even when they weren't together—when Ruger was involved in a carving contest or in discussion with a potential buyer—even that was wonderful for Talli. Just watching Ruger carve was mesmerizing. Of course, as Ruger delighted in teasingly reminding her, Talli was charged with taking care of his phone while he was carving—lest some sort of radioactive leakage be heaped upon him at keeping his phone in his front pocket while he was working and irreparable damage be done to his reproductive capabilities. Naturally, Talli blushed every time Ruger would reference her apparent concern for him the day they'd met—which only seemed to spur the sexy chainsaw carver to making certain he teased her about it again the next time the opportunity presented itself. But Talli loved Ruger's teasing her—loved his kissing her here and there right out in the open—loved Ruger!

And as superb as that first day spent with Ruger at the fiesta was, the first evening was even more magnificent.

Ruger's brother Colt had an RV parked in a space allotted for vendors near the field. And once both Ruger and Talli had downloaded the copious contents of their memory cards, they'd headed back out to the field for the balloon glow. Instead of wandering around—in and out of the inflated balloons that lit up sporadically, looking like enormous, soft-yellow light bulbs as the pilots laid on their burners to "glow" their tethered balloons as everyone else there did—Ruger had found a fabulous spot to sit someway off from the main event, and Talli enjoyed the isolation. Besides, she knew watching the glow from a distance was an entirely different experience than being in the very midst of it, albeit just as enchanting.

Ruger had sat down with his back against a concrete table and then pulled Talli into the warmth and protection of his body as she settled between his knees. There they'd lingered, for over two hours, just watching the balloons and the people, talking quietly and trading sometimes soft, sometimes intimate kisses, until the balloonists had packed up their envelopes, burners, and baskets and left the field to catch a few hours of sleep before the entire process began again the next morning.

It was all like lingering in a daydream—or at least starring in a great rom-com movie—and Talli wished it could never end, wished neither she nor Ruger would ever have to work the funnel cake and breakfast burrito stands for the rest of the fiesta, never have to return to real life and real jobs and real schedules after it was over.

Yet it wasn't just their first day together at the fiesta that was so fantastic but every balloon fiesta day afterward—every day for the remainder of the entire week and weekend that was heaven to Talli. Even when she was working making, serving, and selling funnel cake, it was wonderful! For Ruger was just across the way making, serving, or selling breakfast burritos. Thus, whenever missing him seemed unendurable—whenever Talli began to think her shift would never end and she'd never be in charge of Ruger's phone while he was carving or linger in his arms as the sun set over the West Mesa or feel his fabulous, delicious, hot, and moist kiss again—she could simply glance over to the Villarreal's burrito stand and gaze at him longingly—watch him until he looked up to smile at her and toss her a chin-thrust and a wink, silently reminding her that their shifts would be over soon and they could be together.

And when their shifts did end and they were finally together, Talli was always somewhat astonished at how she and Ruger fell right into easy conversation, as if they'd been a couple for most of their lives instead of merely days—a week—a splendid, romance-filled week that flew by exactly as if it were on fast forward.

♥

It was the last day of the Albuquerque International Balloon Fiesta—at least for another year. Talli always simultaneously loved and hated the last day. She loved the last day for the fact that she was worn out from being up so early every morning—and pretty much sick of funnel cake. She loved it because the bulk of October still remained—still three weeks of October bliss to enjoy. But she did hate the last day of fiesta too—hated that the huge congregation of balloons was gone for another year. There were hot air balloons aloft many mornings in Albuquerque throughout the entirety of every year—and Talli loved every single one of them! But it wasn't the same as witnessing hundreds upon hundreds of the colorful jewels drifting over the North Valley and the Rio Grande River or past one's window each morning that first week in October. Therefore, Talli knew that once the fireworks display was over that night, ending the balloon fiesta for the year, that unwelcome yet familiar letdown feeling would wash over her.

Still, she and Ruger were both off that afternoon and evening—no frying funnel cakes, no rolling breakfast burritos. Additionally, Ruger wasn't carving at all that last day. That meant the afternoon and evening were theirs to enjoy as they chose, and Ruger and Talli had agreed to suck every ounce of fun out of the last day of the fiesta that they could.

Consequently, as the balloonists began returning to the field in preparation for the final balloon glow of the year, Ruger and Talli meandered together over the field talking and trying to absorb as much of the atmosphere as they could.

"The pilots and crews all look wiped out," Ruger quietly pointed out as he and Talli strolled past the crews of the three Little Bees special shapes balloons.

"Yeah, they do," Talli whispered in return. "If I'm this worn out after selling funnel cake for just half a day here and there, I can't imagine how worn out these guys all are."

"I know, huh. I really enjoy the balloons…but I don't love them enough to do it," Ruger admitted.

"Me neither," Talli said—although sleep deprivation wasn't her personal reason for not wanting to be an actual balloonist, or even ride in one for that matter.

For Talli, the danger wasn't worth the risk. As she and Ruger had discussed earlier in the week, hot air ballooning was dangerous. Having both grown up in Albuquerque—having lingered in and around the balloons for their entire lives—Ruger and Talli both owned memories of tragic hot air ballooning accidents. Neither one of them had been close at hand during one, thankfully. But both had seen the newscasts. Fatalities often resulted from the worst ballooning accidents, and although serious accidents were rare and fatalities even rarer, Talli Chaucer had never held a desire to actually ride in one of the glorious drifting things she so loved to watch and photograph.

"Well, hello, you two!"

Kimber's voice jogged Talli's thoughts away from the worrisome side of ballooning and back to the moment.

Turning, Talli found herself face to face with not only Kimber Villarreal but also another young woman in her company. Kimber held a plate with the remains of a funnel cake on it; her friend, a large bowl of tortilla chips slathered in melted nacho cheese and topped with jalapeños.

"Hello, Ruger," the woman with Kimber said.

If Talli had had feathers, they would've been ruffled—for the woman with Kimber was eyeing Ruger up like he was a big juicy steak and she'd been on a kale and liquid cleanse for a year!

"Kimber. Sophia," Ruger greeted, frowning. "What are you guys doing here?"

Kimber raised herself on her tiptoes, planting an affectionate kiss to Ruger's cheek. Laughing a little, she answered, "What do you mean? It's a free country, isn't it? We came by to see the last glow and enjoy a couple of Colt's burritos." Kimber winked at Talli, adding, "And a funnel cake too." Returning her attention to Ruger, she asked, "Are you carving tonight or no? We were going to watch you."

"I was looking forward to watching you again this year, Ruger. But your name isn't on the list for carving tonight," the girl named Sophia said, seductively running one index finger from Ruger's right shoulder to his elbow.

Ruger moved his arm away before Sophia's finger could continue any farther past his elbow, however.

"Too bad, I guess," he said.

"And this must be Talli," Sophia said, looking to Talli then.

Even though Sophia smiled at her, Talli could read the expression of envy and resentment in the young woman's eyes.

"Hi, I'm Sophia," Sophia said. "Want a nacho?"

As Sophia held her bowl heaping with chips and cheese toward Talli, Talli smiled, shook her head, and said, "Thanks, but we've been eating our way through the fiesta all week, and I'm way overloaded."

Sophia's forced, friendly smile faded ever so slightly, but the spitfire in her dark eyes made Talli extra glad she'd refused the offer of a nacho. Sophia looked exactly like the kind of beauty that could be lethal—the kind that might put rat poison in some nachos and then offer it to her competition.

Shrugging, Sophia selected a nacho herself, raising it to her perfectly lined, perfectly lipsticked mouth and taking a small bite.

"Are you guys just planning to hang until the glow or what?" Kimber asked Talli.

"Yeah," Talli assured her. "We're kind of tired. You know how the last day of the fiesta is."

Talli had had two more encounters with Kimber Villarreal since their first meeting at Dion's the previous weekend. Each had been uncomfortable, of course, but not as uncomfortable as their first—and Talli was glad. She didn't want an enemy in Ruger's sister—not when her heart was certain Kimber would one day be her sister-in-law. And for that reason, she was glad Kimber seemed to be less hostile toward her.

"Yeah, you guys must be tired," Kimber said, feigning compassion. "All that burrito and funnel cake making. And all that making out in Colt's RV in between, huh."

"That's right," Ruger said.

"So...what I saw last weekend wasn't a one-time thing then, Ruger?" Sophia said then, her smile completely fading.

"Absolutely not," Ruger answered.

Talli gritted her teeth, irritated with the girls' intrusion. Ruger had told Talli that it was Sophia who had seen them together the first day of the fiesta—Sophia who had put Kimber on their trail, culminating with Kimber's showing up at Dion's their first night together. Therefore, Talli had already decided Sophia Montoya was an enemy. Having to stand there being cordial with a woman she knew was jealous was frustrating.

"Don't you know, Soph?" Kimber began. "Talli's thee one. The one Ruger's been—" She paused to make quotation marks with her free hand. "—saving himself for."

"What?" Sophia squeaked with sudden heightened emotion. Her dark eyes narrowed as she glared at Ruger. "I thought you only met this chick last weekend."

"Well, officially, yeah," Ruger said.

Sophia sneered a moment before smiling again—a smile thick with disgusted disbelief.

"Unreal," she said.

Sophia twisted the wrist of her hand holding the bowl of nachos so that her hand, wrist, and arm formed a catapult of sorts, and Talli gasped when she launched the bowl in her direction.

Talli closed her eyes, certain she was about to be smacked in the face with warm cheese and tortilla chips. But when she heard Ruger swear under his breath, she opened her eyes to see that he had somehow managed to step in front of her, taking the bowl of nachos to the chest in order to protect Talli from taking them to the face.

"Are you freaking kidding me, Sophia?" Ruger exclaimed in appalled anger. "I swear, Kimber, you need to think about who you choose to call a friend, you know?"

It took every ounce of self-control Ruger possessed to keep from verbally gnashing Sophia to the bone. She'd stood there on the balloon field and attempted to smash her damn nachos in Talli's face! And although he was very thankful he'd managed to take the hit himself, he was furious.

Kimber, for her part, stood with her mouth gaping open, seemingly as astonished as Talli appeared to be. But Ruger didn't care; he'd had it with his sister and her beeotch of a friend.

Inhaling a deep breath in to calm himself, Ruger quickly stripped off the T-shirt he'd been wearing.

"Kimber, you and Sophia better turn around and just walk away," he growled as he shook the nachos, cheese, and jalapeños from his shirt onto the grass beneath his feet.

"Ruger, you can't blame me for—" Kimber began.

Raising an index finger and pointing it in her face, he said, "The company you keep says a lot about you too, Kimber. Leave."

As Ruger thought about strangling Sophia with his soiled T-shirt a moment, Sophia looked at him, grinned, and said, "Wow, Ruger. I forgot how stacked you are, babe."

"Kimber, I mean it," Ruger managed to say through teeth that were clenched so hard, they felt like they might crack. "Walk away."

He didn't want to go off at Kimber there; it wasn't the time or place. And he wanted to reassure Talli that he knew it.

"Come on, Sophia," Kimber finally said. "Don't poke the beast any more. He'll tear you apart if you do."

Ruger was startled when he felt his nachos-covered T-shirt being snatched from his hands—felt his own eyebrows raise in astonishment and his clenched jaw relax a bit as he watched Talli toss the T-shirt at Sophia.

Catching it was a reflex for Sophia. But it was what Talli said that pleased Ruger to the tips of his angry toes.

"Here you go," Talli said. "Take that home as my little gift to you. It's the closest you'll ever get to touching my man again, vata."

"Come on, Soph," Kimber said. "We better go."

Ruger wasn't proud of himself for it, but he enjoyed seeing Kimber slink away with her tail between her legs.

And Sophia showed just how classy she truly was not by extending one middle finger in his direction as she tossed his shirt to the ground before she turned and joined Kimber in retreat. If Talli hadn't taken hold of his arm to stay him, he wasn't so sure he could've kept from giving Sophia a good tongue-whipping.

Nevertheless, his entire insides were swelling with pride, elation, and encouragement: Talli had stepped up to Sophia herself. Sure, he'd kept the nachos from hitting their intended mark, but Talli was the one who put the final burn on Sophia with the whole T-shirt thing.

"Vata even!" he chuckled, taking Talli in his arms and kissing her square on the mouth.

Damn, he loved kissing Talli! She was like some smoothie recipe the angels had come up with! And she felt so good in his arms, like she was made to fit there—to fit against his body like he'd been molded to hold her.

"Come on," he said, forcing himself to stop kissing her. "Colt usually has some Villarreal T-shirts on hand at the burrito stand. I don't want to look like an idiot standing out here half dressed."

"You could never look like an idiot," Talli said, smiling up at him. "And I'm sure every woman who can see you right now is thinking she just got a balloon fiesta super bonus."

Kissing her on the forehead just because he loved her and loved the way she exaggerated about how good-looking she thought he was all the time, Ruger tucked Talli under his arm.

"But seriously…can I get, like, a ticket for this? Being out on the field with no shirt?" he asked as they began to walk back toward Vendors' Row.

"Maybe for distracting from the balloons with your hotness is all," she answered.

Again Ruger chuckled. He felt as if his life were only just beginning—as if every moment he'd lived up to the moment he first spoke to Talli hadn't really meant much at all. She was already his entire world. Eight days into meeting her and she was his entire world.

♥

Talli tried once more to avert her eyes—to keep from gawking at Ruger as he stood in the RV going through Colt's closet in search of a shirt to wear for the rest of the day.

"No wonder Colt didn't have any T-shirts left at the stand," Ruger said as he yanked a shirt off a hanger. "They're all in here."

She couldn't keep from looking at him again. She just couldn't! He was unreal. Beeotch that she was, Sophia had been right on the money—Ruger was stacked! Every muscle in his shoulders, chest, arms, abs—his entire torso was...well, magnificent was the word that kept running through Talli's mind.

"Small?" Ruger grumbled, tossing the T-shirt he'd just removed from a hanger to the nearby RV table. "Who in our family wears a small, right?"

"Right?" Talli echoed, for lack of anything else to say.

Ruger glanced to her just then, and she felt her cheeks blush hot and crimson.

"What?" he asked as his handsome brows knit together. "You're looking at me like I'm sprouting warts."

"Oh...um...no. I just know you want to find a shirt and..." Talli stammered, feeling her cheeks burning even worse.

Ruger stepped closer to where she stood then. "Are you jumpy because I'm naked?" he asked, a grin slowly spreading across his face.

"Of course not!" Talli defended herself too defensively. "I mean...I have brothers, you know."

"You are. You're jumpy because I'm naked," Ruger said, reaching out and wrapping her in his arms.

"You're not naked, and I'm not jumpy," Talli assured him, giggling.

But in truth, of course she was nervous! She'd been nervous since the moment he'd stripped his shirt off on the balloon field! Oh sure, shirtless men weren't a novelty. Men ran around without their shirts all the time. But not all men looked like Ruger did without his shirt on. Not all men looked like Ruger anyway! But when he'd stripped off his shirt and revealed what was beneath, Talli's eyes had nearly popped out of her head! She had been so grateful that Ruger was too distracted by Sophia and Kimber to notice Talli's mouth fall agape in awe for a moment. But now—now that she was alone with him in Colt's RV—yeah! She was nervous!

"Well, you don't need to be uncomfortable or jumpy or whatever with me, baby…even if I am naked," Ruger said in a lowered voice. "Didn't you hear my sister? I'm saving myself. And even though I've found you—the one I've been saving myself for—I'll wait until we're married before I do anything too scandalous. You know that, right?"

Instantly Talli felt her body relax against Ruger's. She did know it! And that, coupled with the fact that he had, yet again, referred to their being married one day, was all the reassurance Talli needed.

"That vata was right, you know," she said, gazing up into the eternity of his emerald eyes.

"What do you mean?" Ruger mumbled, pressing a warm kiss to her lips.

"You really are stacked," Talli whispered.

"Hey, you've already got me where you want me," Ruger said. "You can quit with the flattery now."

"I'm only speaking the truth," Talli breathed the moment before Ruger's mouth claimed hers.

Talli's hands seem to be guiding themselves as they slowly, caressively slid up and over the contours of Ruger's broad chest and shoulders—around to the back of his neck. His skin was warm—smooth—and the sense of it against her palms, against her arms—the feel of his whiskers on her face as his mouth worked to rain an incommunicable physical and emotional bliss over her—caused her to begin to tremble in his arms.

Warm and moist, with a flavor that was unique only to him, Ruger's kiss besieged Talli with such an intense love and longing, she wondered how she had ever existed without it! And his touch was just as affecting to her. Whether his hands were at her waist as they were at that moment—as he pushed her gently back against one inner wall of the RV—or whether he was cradling her face in the strength of his palms or tucking a stray strand of hair behind her ear, his touch caused goose bumps to race in successive waves over her arms and legs.

"Have I said it yet?" he mumbled against her mouth.

"S-said what?" she gasped.

"I love you, Talli," Ruger breathed. "I've loved you for so long...and just didn't realize it until that day at the park entrance. I didn't realize I'd been falling in love with you one week a year for the past five years."

As tears sprung to her eyes—tears of immeasurable joy—Talli breathed, "I've been loving you all that time too. I love you so much, Ruger."

"Even when I'm all the way dressed?" he teased.

"Yes, you dork," Talli giggled.

"Good," he mumbled before renewing his adulation of her by way of enrapturing her with his profound, proficient, positively sublime kiss.

CHAPTER TEN

Absolute perfection: sharing nachos with Ruger, sitting in the stands of the University of New Mexico football stadium, watching the UNM Lobos whoop up on the Boise State Broncos. At least to Talli's way of thinking. The warm October sun coupled with the fresh, crisp atmosphere of autumn was ideal football weather, and the aroma of stadium hot dogs, nachos, and popcorn lent a sense of comfort to the air. The clear blue New Mexico sky overhead soothed a soul into almost forgetting there was something other than beauty in the world.

As Talli popped a tortilla chip caked with nacho cheese and heaping with jalapeños into her mouth, she mused aloud, "I wonder what it is about stadium food that makes it so delicious. I mean, these aren't the greatest nachos in the world...and yet they are. You know?"

"I do know," Ruger agreed, dunking a tortilla chip into the deep accumulation of nacho cheese in one corner of the tray of nachos he held. Putting it in his mouth, he moaned. "Mmmm. I love that they use the small chips. One chip, one bite—just the way I like it."

Talli nodded and selected another tortilla chip. "And the cheap cheese. It's, like, so much better than the expensive stuff. I'd take a number ten can of this stuff any day over the little jars you get of the con queso that's supposed to be better."

"Absolutely," Ruger agreed. He picked a jalapeño off the mound heaped in another corner of the nachos tray. "This is what life is all about—nachos with cheap cheese, eating outside in October, and, most of all, being with you."

Talli smiled, leaned forward, and kissed Ruger on one cheek.

"Flattery will get you everywhere, Ruger," she giggled.

"I'm just speaking the truth," he chuckled.

The football game was over, but the elated Lobo fans were taking their time in exiting the stands—basking in their Lobo's triumph over Boise State's Broncos. Ruger and Talli were lingering as well. For one thing, they had an order of nachos to finish. And for another, Ruger was right: there was nothing quite like late afternoon in October. It was a carefree sensation—one to be soaked up and savored.

To Talli, the first week back to regular work after the balloon fiesta had seemed to drag on and on. Not that Talli didn't enjoy her job—she did. Being an esthetician, Talli took pleasure in the fact that people often arrived for an appointment feeling stressed out but left feeling more relaxed and positive about life in general once she had worked her magic. Consequently, it hadn't been the actual work that had made the week feel long; it was the separation from Ruger during the day.

Having spent almost every waking hour with him during the fiesta—or at least gazing across the way at him while they each worked their vendor stands—Talli found that the reality of needing to earn a living dampened every weekday since. Sure, they saw each other every day after work and hung out together late—into the early morning hours most nights. But sleep deprivation and the necessity of having a career were wearing. Especially when all Talli wanted to do was be with Ruger—every minute.

But spending a bright, sunny Saturday with him at the Lobo football game proved to chase away the wretchedness of the workday separation. And even though the sun was beginning to slip lower and lower into the west, indicating that the day would soon be over, Talli was bathed in bliss, for she was with Ruger, and Monday morning was still a way off.

"I was thinking we should ride the tram tonight," Ruger suggested, dipping a chip.

"Ooo, yeah! There's not a cloud in the sky, so there'll be a clear view of the city lights when the sun goes down," Talli agreed with excitement.

"I know the restaurant is closed up there—they're renovating it or something—but we can get dinner when we come back down if you want," Ruger said.

"Oh, I'm not worried about dinner," Talli giggled, "not after a mountain of these bad boys." She nodded toward the tray of quickly vanishing nachos Ruger still held.

It was funny the way Ruger was always thinking about food, even when he was in the process of eating. But Talli knew the hot burrito guy burned a lot of energy, not only working at chainsaw carving but also during his daily workouts. Thus, it was no wonder he seemed to have food on the brain, a lot of the time.

In truth, Talli had learned so much about the man she was in love with during their second, non-fiesta week together. And the more she learned about Ruger Villarreal, the more she fell in love with him! In fact, every night (or rather early morning) when Talli finally fell into bed, she drifted to sleep knowing she could never love Ruger more than she already did. And yet, come the next day and more time spent with him, she loved him more! Talli often wondered how she had found any joy in life at all before she'd met Ruger. And she couldn't imagine going further through life without him. It was fascinating to her, the way they'd met that day at the fiesta entrance—the way life had propelled them forward, together.

Talli had been so nervous when, only a couple of days after the end of the fiesta, Ruger had insisted she meet his entire family, at a dinner his parents had hosted to enable Ruger to introduce Talli to the family. She'd been so afraid that other members of the Villarreal family would feel averse toward her the way Kimber obviously did. But every one of Ruger's siblings welcomed her with opened arms— literally. Even Kimber had apologized to Talli for being such a "beeotch" at first, and for Sophia's behavior as well. And although Talli could still sense that Kimber wasn't as trusting of her as Ruger's other siblings, she was nice to Talli—sincerely encouraging to Talli and Ruger as a couple.

Ruger's parents assured Talli that if their son felt he'd found his Mrs. Right, then they trusted in his judgment. Ruger's dad had even whisked Talli aside at the family dinner and assured her that, had any of his other children claimed they'd fallen in love at first sight, he would've owned extreme concern. But Ruger wasn't like any of Mr. Villarreal's other children. If Ruger said he'd found the woman he'd been looking for his whole life—if Ruger said he'd recognized Talli as that woman the moment they'd met—than Mr. Villarreal believed him. It was more encouraging than Talli could've ever imagined—the fact that Ruger's entire family (even Kimber) was so accepting and kind to Talli.

Talli's family was likewise as accepting of Ruger as the Villarreals had been of Talli. Other than a background check or two performed by her brothers, the Chaucers jumped right into thinking of Ruger as

Talli's boyfriend—her serious boyfriend. At first, it seemed strange to Talli that both families would be so easily accepting. But as Ruger pointed out, both he and Talli came from close, communicative families, and communicative families tended to trust one another.

And so Talli had been able to discard any residual doubt or worry she'd still had where Ruger's intentions were concerned, and she'd run headlong into planning on spending the rest of her life with him.

♥

"It's weird how you tend to not appreciate the cool things you have in your hometown, you know?" Ruger commented as he pulled into a parking spot in the Sandia Peak Aerial Tramway parking lot.

The sun was setting, and Talli fixed her gaze on the beautiful Sandia Mountains looming before them.

"You mean like the tram and the way the mountains turn hot pink for just a couple of minutes at sunset?" Talli responded.

"Yeah," Ruger said. He turned off the engine of his truck and relaxed against his seat.

Talli smiled as she gazed at him. She knew why he was pausing in getting out of the truck; it was the same reason she was. In a moment or two more, it would happen—the miracle of nature that Talli had adored and marveled at for as long as she could remember. As the sun set in the west, casting its last and most brilliant rays of the day over the face of Sandia Mountains, the mountains themselves would appear to soak up the light—appear to blush hot pink with wanting to keep the sun from setting. It was the very reason the Sandia Mountains were so named—Sandia, the Spanish word for watermelon. And there could not have been a more perfect description of the wondrous transformation of the mountains just before sunset than to refer to them as watermelon, for that's exactly what the Sandia looked like in those brief but wondrous moments at the end of the day. The mountain did indeed look like a giant slice of deep pink watermelon.

"Here she goes," Ruger said as he and Talli both stared up at the mass of rock and trees and beauty before them.

"I love this," Talli sighed as the mountain turned fuchsia right before her eyes. It wouldn't last long, perhaps two minutes. But it would be a glorious, awe-inspiring two minutes!

"It never fails to give me pause, you know? To amaze me," Ruger said, in a low, mesmerized tone.

"Me neither," Talli agreed quietly. "I did a project on the Sandia in high school. It's the potassium-feldspar crystals embedded in the granite of the mountain that give it the pink when the sun hits them just right at sunset."

"I did not know that," Ruger said, smiling at Talli.

Talli giggled, shrugged, and said, "I didn't either. When I was a kid, I just thought it was magic."

"It is magic," Ruger chuckled, "just helped along by potassium-feldspar...whatever that is."

Talli laughed, and Ruger felt warmed all over. He loved her laugh! It was like a zillion endorphins flooded his body whenever she laughed. To Ruger, Talli's laugh was the most beautiful sound a person could ever hear.

And as he sat there in his pickup with her—as he watched her eyes flash with admiration at the display of one of nature's most beautiful miracles unfolding before them—he made up his mind. He'd been considering doing it all day anyway. But now he was sure, and to hell with what anybody else thought. This was between him and Talli, and hadn't he waited two weeks already? Two weeks from today was the day they'd officially met—the day Talli had biffed it on the pavement in front of him (he winced at the memory of her scraped and bleeding chin) and the opportunity had finally been presented to meet her. Two weeks. To Ruger it seemed like it had been two years! So enough messing around. After all, two weeks was plenty of time, time enough for both Talli's family and his own to get used to the idea—the idea that he and Talli were meant for one another, meant to be married.

And besides, he'd been carrying the damn ring around in his pocket for days. It was time he put it on Talli's finger so he didn't have to worry about losing it.

"And just like that…it's over for another day," Ruger said as the watermelon pink faded into a purple-mountains-majesty indigo orchid.

"Yep," Talli sighed, feeling a bit let down. To go from brilliant fuchsia to violet blue was a disappointment to her no matter what the subject was. But when the Sandia Mountains faded in the evening, it signaled the end of the day for sure, and that meant it would soon be the end of her time with Ruger—at least until the next evening.

"You still wanna go up?" Ruger asked.

Talli looked to him to see he wore an expression of doubting she was still up for the tram.

"Of course I do!" she assured him. "There's nothing I like more than hanging by a thread. I especially love the part where they tell you that if the cable broke right then, it would take eight seconds for the tramcar to hit the ground. Have you ever counted out eight seconds? It's forever! I mean…if you're anticipating death, it's forever."

Ruger laughed and shook his head. "Maybe I better consider whether or not I still want to go," he teased.

"Come on, hot stuff," Talli giggled. "Let's go hang by a thread together. What do you say?"

"I say we go for it," Ruger answered with a nod of affirmation.

The Sandia Peak Tram was one of Albuquerque's most popular tourist draws. Beginning at the foothills of the Sandia Mountains, the tram traveled four thousand feet along the western face of the Sandia to an observation deck and Sandia Peak Ski Area perched above ten thousand feet. The view from the mountain's crest was incredible—taking in eleven thousand square miles of New Mexico's enchanting landscape, including the city of Albuquerque nestled in the valley below. Talli especially loved viewing Albuquerque's valley and the west side's dormant volcanoes and lava-based mesas from the crest as the sun set and afterward. Although tourists loved the tram for the unique attraction it was, locals loved it simply because it was awe-inspiring and downright cool. It wasn't necessarily something native New Mexicans did often—more something to do when a body just wanted to literally rise above the stresses of the day, treat visitors, or simply enjoy it just for the heck of it once every few years.

For Talli's part, she hadn't ridden the tram for at least a couple of years, and the idea of being at the top of the crest after sundown in October was exhilarating. The lights of Albuquerque were beautiful from the crest at night, and to share that with Ruger—well, what could be more romantic?

There hadn't been a significant wait to ride the tram. Soon Talli found herself standing in the middle of the tramcar holding onto one of the poles in the center of the car. Ruger was standing behind her as he held the pole with one hand, his other lingering at her waist at the front.

"And from this point," the young man escorting the tramcar up in to order provide information began, "it would take eight seconds to reach the ground…if anyone decided to exit the tramcar for some reason."

A low, nervous chuckle rumbled through the tramcar—passengers chortling with either anxious anticipation at the thought or mild amusement at those who were anxious at the thought.

"That's the part I hate knowing," Talli whispered.

"Here, don't think about it," Ruger mumbled against her ear. "Think about how awesome that little old couple over there is." Ruger nodded toward the elderly couple sitting on the east end of the tram, looking through the window toward the crest.

Ruger had given his seat up when the silver-haired man and woman had stepped onto the tramcar. He'd kindly insisted that the woman have his seat. Of course, wanting to stand by Ruger anyway, Talli had quickly followed suit, offering the man her seat, explaining that she wanted to stand by Ruger.

Now she stood, wrapped in Ruger's arms, as they both gazed with admiration at the couple who sat holding hands and watching the tramcar ascend toward the crest.

"That'll be us in fifty years, you know," Ruger said. "Me and you, just out for a night to ride the ol' Sandia Peak Tramway, for no other reason than we want to be together."

"You mean, just like tonight then," Talli said, leaning back against the firm contours of his chest.

"Yep. Just like tonight," Ruger agreed.

It was only fifteen minutes from the tramcar dock to the dock at the top of the mountain. But Talli still felt relieved to have firm ground—or rather deck wood—under her feet again. She was also glad Ruger always carried extra coats and sweatshirts in his truck, because the temperature at the top of the Sandia was much, much lower than it had been at the foothills. Still, with one of Ruger's barn coats over her own sweatshirt, Talli felt warm enough.

Walking along the boardwalk, past the old restaurant that was now under reconstruction, and to a favorite lookout spot, Talli breathed in the cold night air.

"This is my favorite place up here," she told Ruger as they stood gazing out over the valley of Albuquerque.

"Mine too," Ruger said, moving to stand behind her and wrapping his arms around her.

As he placed a warm, moist kiss to her neck just below her ear, Talli sighed with contentment. Below them, Albuquerque looked like a literal river of lights! Many photographers attempted to capture the wonder of the lights of Albuquerque as viewed from the top of the Sandia Mountains. But Talli had yet to see a photograph that could even begin to capture the wonder of it. It was a breathtaking sight— an indescribable view! A stripe of dark red hovered over the volcanoes to the west, the last crimson blush the sun left in its wake, and against that crimson stripe loomed the dark silhouette of the volcanoes in front of it. Yet in the foreground—on the magical space of canvas between the mountains to the east of the city and the volcanoes to the west—twinkled the otherworldly lights of Albuquerque. Oh, the lights of Albuquerque were famous to anyone who had come upon them at night—especially those traveling east from west of the city. But the view from atop the Sandia's crest was a marvel in itself. One felt as if he or she were hovering over an enchantment of lights and movement. It was a truly breathtaking view, and Talli stood in awe of it—in awe of the sparkling beauty below and before her and in awe of the man who was holding her in his arms, sharing that view.

"Well, you two look like you're having a good time."

Talli looked away from the city below to see the elderly couple she and Ruger had given up their tramcar seats for.

"Oh, we are. Thank you, sir," Ruger confirmed.

"It's a bit cold up here this evening," the elderly woman said to Talli. "I wasn't expecting to see so much snow yet."

"I know, huh?" Talli agreed.

"Are you two up here for an occasion? Or just for fun?" Ruger asked.

"Oh, we come up here every six months or so," the old gentleman said. "We were married up here—almost right on this spot, sixty-five years ago this past summer."

"Wow!" Talli heard herself exclaim in unison with Ruger.

"That's wonderful!" Talli added. And she truly was astonished to hear that the couple had been married so very long—astonished and delighted.

The little old lady dropped her voice as she said, "We just saw another young couple up here, a ways over there." She laughed a little under her breath. "Poor little thing! She's wearing one of these dresses that looks like someone just tied a piece of elastic around her, a pair of those eight-inch platform heels—and her teeth were chattering to beat the band. Bless her heart, I don't think she knew her boyfriend was bringing her up to the crest tonight."

"Oh, how awful," Talli said, her own concerned expression matching that of the old woman's.

"Now you…you two show some sense and know-how," the man said, "dressed proper for the occasion." The old man winked at Ruger, adding, "Your girl knows she can trust you to take care of her no matter what. That's what I see."

"That's right, sir," Ruger said, kissing Talli on one cheek.

Talli smiled, warmed by his kiss—by being held in his arms—not to mention the fact that Ruger had been prepared for anything, even and including a spontaneous tram ride.

"Well, we best be lettin' you two get back to necking," the old man said.

The old woman playfully smacked her husband on one shoulder. "Harold!" she scolded.

But the old man laughed. "Well, I figure he's got the same designs on his pretty little filly that I've got on mine, Mary." He winked at Ruger and then took his wife's hand and began leading her farther down the boardwalk.

"You two have a nice evening now," Mary called over one shoulder.

"Thank you, ma'am. You too," Ruger called after the sweet old couple.

It was time. They couldn't linger there on the observation deck too much longer. As bundled up as she was, Ruger could feel the cold on Talli's face. Jack Frost came early to the crest, and he was already nipping at Talli's nose. And besides, Ruger's guts were shivering—not from the cold but from nervous anticipation. What if he was wrong? What if Talli wasn't ready to commit to forever with him? And yet Ruger knew by the way she looked at him, by the way she smiled at him and responded to his touch. She was as ready as he was.

Briefly the thought, But what will people think? It's only been two weeks! pricked at his brain. But it was only a brief prick.

"Screw you guys. I hate high school," Ruger heard himself whisper.

"What?" Talli asked Ruger. He'd muttered something under his breath, but she hadn't been able to hear exactly what he'd said.

"So, Talli…" Ruger began.

"Yeah?" Talli encouraged with a giggle.

"How long have we known each other?"

Talli giggled again. Turning in Ruger's arms, she put her own arms around his neck, kissing him softly on the mouth.

"Our souls have known each other forever," she answered, smiling.

"True," Ruger agreed. He grinned as he gazed down at her. "But I meant, officially."

"Two weeks," Talli answered. "Actually, several hours more than two weeks…depending on what time it is right now."

"Also true," Ruger affirmed, his grin broadening to a smile. "And we even have a song."

"We do!" Talli quietly exclaimed. "A wonderful, romantic, totally retro song!"

Again Ruger laughed. "And even though my hair isn't as badass as Barry Gibbs's…I'm pretty sure you love me."

"Your hair is so much sexier than Barry Gibbs's," Talli said, running her fingers up the back of Ruger's neck and into his hair.

Talli loved Ruger's playfulness—the way he sometimes needed reassurance that she was totally in love with him, even though she felt it was obvious.

"Why, thank you, Miss Chaucer," Ruger chuckled.

He kissed her then—pressed a warm, moist, and wonderful kiss to her mouth—as he began to sway a little as he held her in his arms.

Oh, how had she been so lucky? Why had heaven chosen to grant Talli her wildest dream come true? How did it all happen? Was she really there, standing on the Sandia crest on a cold October night, kissing the man she loved more than her own life, as the lights of Albuquerque twinkled below them? For a moment, Ruger's incredibly delicious kiss caused Talli to feel dizzy—to wonder if the lights shimmering below in the valley were really the stars in heaven and everything—the entire world—had just flipped upside down.

"So you love me, and we have song," Ruger mumbled against her mouth.

"Yes?" Talli breathed.

"And I love you, and after all...we waited two weeks, right?"

Talli pulled away from Ruger, but only far enough to look at his expression.

"We've waited two weeks for what?" she asked, still rather dizzy from his kisses.

"For this."

It took Talli several moments to realize what Ruger's intention was as, while taking hold of her left hand, he knelt down on one knee in front of her.

She stopped breathing! She literally could not breathe as she watched him reach into his front pocket with his free hand.

With some assistance from the lights of the tramcar dock some distance off, the moonlight fell to the beautiful diamond solitaire Ruger was holding toward her, causing a flash so brilliant, anyone nearby to witness it may have well thought a star had fallen from the clear New Mexico sky to land exactly in his hand.

"I bought this three days after we met...after we officially met," Ruger said.

As tears filled Talli's eyes—as her heart began to race so quickly, to beat so fast she thought she might faint—he continued.

"And I've waited as long as I can stand to wait to ask you something." He paused, an expression passing over his face that spoke of momentary doubt—fear of rejection.

"Talli…will you marry me?" Ruger asked. "And if you will…will you please do it sooner than later?"

She didn't pause—for what reason was there to pause?

"Of course!" Talli cried out louder than she had intended. "Of course and of course!"

She felt the warmth of the ring and Ruger's hand as he slipped the ring onto her left ring finger—the place where it would stay forever.

Standing to his full height once more, Ruger took Talli's face between his strong hands, grinding such a kiss of passionate possession to her mouth, Talli had to stiffen her knees to keep from collapsing.

"I love you, Talli the funnel cake girl," Ruger breathed once he'd kissed her to near unconsciousness.

"I love you, Ruger the sexy burrito boy," Talli whispered, tears of joy streaming over her cheeks.

Talli held her hand up close to her face—studied the beautiful ring Ruger had put on her finger.

"You bought this three days after we met?" she asked, smiling.

"I most certainly did," Ruger affirmed.

"But…but aren't you worried about what people will think?" she asked. "I mean, it's only been two weeks and—"

"It seems like an eternity to me, baby," Ruger explained, taking her hand in his and kissing the back of it. "Our business is our business. Our timetable is our timetable."

"I know," Talli assured him. She smiled as she caressed his whiskery cheek with her hand. "And besides, it's like my brothers always say—'Screw you guys. I hate—'"

But Ruger's ravenous kiss interrupted her words as he proceeded to bathe her in such a surreal and overpowering passion, Talli was certain she would never recover—and absolutely did not care if she didn't.

The fresh, crisp air of an Albuquerque October filled Talli's lungs, and the lights of Albuquerque glittered below as the stars twinkled above. But in those moments—those wonderful, enchanting moments as Talli stood wrapped in the loving strength of Ruger's arms—his ring on her finger and his mouth blending with hers—to her there was only her and Ruger in all the world: the funnel cake girl who had somehow won the love of the sexy burrito guy, the love she'd so very long wished for.

EPILOGUE

Talli stood in the parking lot of the balloon fiesta park. It had been an entire year since she'd last savored the feelings—the sight, the sounds, the aromas—the cool, crisp air of a predawn October morning in Albuquerque. Everything she'd so looked forward to greeted her—the perfectly clear yet still-dark sky so seemingly bedazzled with an endless array of silvery stars twinkling overhead. The quiet of the morning was there and the distant scent of oil heating in frying pans, of tortillas being kept fresh and warm in warmers, of green chile, freshly roasted and waiting to tantalize the taste buds of visitors to the Albuquerque International Balloon Fiesta. Yes, everything Talli so loved about October in Albuquerque was there.

And still she found herself having to choke back the tears brimming in her eyes—tears born of mingled joy and melancholy nostalgia. The reality that her years of working at the funnel cake stand were over unexpectedly pinched her heart. As at the same time, the joy she lived every day in knowing the reason she would never work the funnel cake stand again almost overwhelmed her with bliss.

"You okay, baby?" Ruger asked as he stepped up beside her, placing one strong, protective arm around her shoulders as he tucked her safely beneath his arm and against his warm body.

"Yeah," Talli said, smiling up at him. She brushed the two tears from her cheek that had managed to escape and smiled at her sexy chainsaw-carving husband. "Just kind of back and forth with emotions today, you know?" She giggled, adding, "Hormones bouncing around, I suppose," as Ruger kissed the top of her head with reassurance.

"Well, you know we'll be back every day that you want to come, every year for the rest of our lives, right?" Ruger offered. "The only difference is you won't have to make the funnel cake. You can just eat it!"

"I know, huh?" Talli said, brushing another fugitive tear from her cheek. "I don't even know why I'm crying," she sniffled. "I truly won't miss working so hard during the festival...not at all. I mean it. And we certainly won't be dragging the baby out here in the cold morning air every day. I suppose I'm just so happy...so excited..." She paused, gazing up into Ruger's handsome face and sighing with admiration and love. "I'm so, so, so in love with you, even more than I was yesterday and the day before...which is an inconceivable notion in itself. And I can't imagine how fabulous it will be to just enjoy the beauty and wonder of fiesta, to watch the balloons for as long as I want without feeling pulled back toward the funnel cake stand...to watch you carve in the competitions and see the look of amazed admiration on people's faces when they see your work."

"And hang onto my phone for me so that my testicles still work," Ruger teased. "Even though we obviously know they work now, right?"

"Well, we want them to continue working, don't we?" Talli teased in return. "We wouldn't want our baby to be an only child, not when his dad and mom were blessed with so many siblings."

Talli and Ruger both laughed, amused at the ridiculous things they found humor in together.

"But honestly, babe, I'm relieved to not be working the stand this year," Talli sighed. "Of course there is one downside to it," she continued, smiling up at Ruger again. "I'll never be able to stare at you from across the fiesta park entrance, to just watch you as you work…to stalk my sexy burrito guy without his knowing while I make funnel cake."

Ruger smiled down at Talli—bent and placed a long, lingering kiss to her mouth. As always, his kiss was warm and moist, laced with loving passion, as well as the lingering flavor of mint toothpaste.

"Be careful here," he said, slipping an arm around her waist. "This is where you biffed it last year, chica."

"Ruger," Talli said, as ever flattered and grateful for his protective nature, "I'm four months pregnant…not nine."

"You still need to be careful," he playfully warned.

"Hey, eses!" Colt called from the burrito stand as Ruger and Talli approached. "You came out to enjoy the festivities as regular civilians, que no?"

"You know it, bro," Ruger said, reaching out to shake hands with his brother over the burrito order counter. "Can we get two with everything?" Ruger asked. He reached into his back pocket and retrieved his wallet, offering Colt a twenty and a ten.

"Two hot chocolates too please, Colt," Talli added.

"You know it, girl," Colt said, smiling at Talli. "Anything for the mommy of my new niece or nephew!" He nodded to Ruger, saying, "And keep your money, bro. What? You think I'd charge you?"

"It's your business, man," Ruger argued, however. "You can't give it away free."

Colt tossed a chin-thrust at his brother and said, "Bring me some funnel cake later, and we'll call it even."

Ruger chuckled, nodded, and said, "All right, bro. All right."

But when Colt turned to call out the order over his shoulder, Ruger reached over the counter and dropped the cash into the open till he knew was there.

Talli's heart swelled with pride in her husband's integrity. Ruger winked at her, and she wrapped her arms around his strong one as he shoved his hand in his front pocket.

"Good morning, guys!" Kimber cheerfully greeted as she appeared from the back room of the stand, tying her cook's apron at her back. "Eee, it's freezing today!" she exclaimed, shivering.

"Oh, you'll warm up soon enough," Ruger encouraged, leaning over the order counter to kiss his sister on the cheek. "You still treating Todd all right, Nineteen-Eleven?"

Kimber rolled her eyes and shook her head. "Yes, Ruger, I'm still treating Todd all right. Very well in fact...the way he deserves to be treated."

"I'm glad to hear it," Ruger stated.

"Híjole!" Kimber exclaimed. "A girl has a couple of rough years, and her brothers never let her live it down."

Kimber winked at Talli, and Talli smiled, glad that Kimber had finally found humility and common sense enough to be someone almost really likeable.

"How're you feeling, Talls?" Kimber asked.

"Much better," Talli answered with a sigh of relief. "No more morning sickness...or saltines."

"Awesome!" Kimber exclaimed sincerely. "Take it easy today though. Don't wear yourself out too much."

"I won't," Talli agreed.

"Order up!" one of Colt's friends who was working the burrito stand called.

"There you go, bro," Colt said, handing two perfectly foil-wrapped breakfast burritos to Ruger. "And just for my sweet sister-in-law…"

Talli giggled as Colt reached to the warming tray next to him, snatching up two sandwich bags of green chile and plopping them on top of the burritos Ruger held.

"Awww, Colt! You remembered!" Talli exclaimed.

"How could I forget? I swear your guys' baby is going to come out looking like a green chile, the way you two eat it," Colt teased.

"Two hot chocolates to go, as well," Kimber said, handing Talli two large Styrofoam, lidded coffee cups with swizzle straws.

"Mmm! Thanks, Kimber," Talli said.

"You two lovebirds have fun not working today," Colt said.

"Hey, I am working today," Ruger reminded his brother.

"Oh, yeah, I forgot—whacking up a piece of wood with a chainsaw so someone will pay fifty grand for it, huh?" Colt joked.

"Eee, I wish," Ruger laughed.

"Well, have fun on your non-working morning, kids," Colt said before he stepped over to the other order window.

"Thanks, Kimber," Talli said as she blew into the small opening in the top of her hot chocolate lid.

"Of course," Kimber said, smiling—sincerely smiling. "See you guys later."

Ruger tossed a chin-thrust to his sister. "Have fun."

Kimber arched one eyebrow in questioning whether her brother meant it to be as sarcastic as he sounded.

"Come on, baby," he said to Talli then. "Let's find a place to really enjoy the dawn patrol launch, hmm?"

"Yeah," Talli agreed.

As she and Ruger slowly ambled toward the balloon field, Ruger stopped short when they reached one of the outlying picnic tables.

"You know what?" he began. "I don't think I've ever—not in all my life—actually sat down to eat a breakfast burrito at the fiesta. Wanna sit?"

"You bet," she agreed.

Talli smiled, her heart warming in knowing that Ruger was simply concerned for her comfort, not his own. He was so wonderful! So caring, so strong and handsome! She couldn't believe they had been married nearly a year. One more month, and she would have been Mrs. Ruger Villarreal for a year! It seemed like a dream—like she was living a dream, which she realized in that moment she actually was. Oh, how she hoped their baby—whether it was a boy or a girl— would make its debut sporting the same gorgeous black hair, olive skin, and green eyes that its daddy did!

As they sat down at the picnic table, Talli shivered a little. Kimber was right! It was a little chillier than Talli had expected. Then again, for all she knew, it was always this chilly the first morning of balloon fiesta—when one wasn't working frying up funnel cake, at least.

Tearing the foil off one end of his burrito, Ruger took a large bite, moaning, "Mmm! I swear these are so much better when you're not having to make them yourself."

"I can well imagine," Talli agreed. "I'm actually looking forward to eating funnel cake this year."

They sat in silence together for a moment—enjoying the hot, savory flavor of a warm flour tortilla stuffed with scrambled eggs, sausage, cheddar cheese, and of course a healthy dose of green chile. The hot chocolate only served to heighten Talli's enjoyment of the combination, and the quiet, crisp darkness of an early October morning in New Mexico was the perfect atmosphere in which to relish the beauty of life.

The slight fluttering feeling she'd been feeling in her abdomen for several days suddenly began again, and Talli smiled—for she was certain of it then, certain it wasn't just the butterflies she usually experienced when enjoying something wonderful with Ruger. It was different, and she knew it.

"I can feel the baby moving," she said quietly to her husband.

Ruger stopped chewing. His eyes widened.

"You mean…like right now?" he asked, his mouth still full of a half-eaten bite of burrito.

"Yeah," Talli assured him. "I wasn't sure at first—you know, over the past few days. I wasn't sure, but just now…just as that third or fourth bite of burrito hit my stomach…"

Talli gazed up into Ruger's shining, emerald eyes.

"It's the baby I'm feeling…I can tell," she whispered.

She watched then as the mesmerizing eyes of the most handsome and wonderful man she could've ever dreamed of belonging to filled with excess moisture. Ruger's happiness was so apparent—so beautiful—and Talli felt tears welling in her own eyes.

Putting his burrito down on the picnic table next to his hot chocolate—and not too gently at that—Ruger took Talli's face between his warm, powerful hands and kissed her with such an obviously emotional manner that Talli's tears escaped her eyes to trickle down over her cheeks.

"A year ago today, querida," he mumbled against her mouth. "A year ago today—the first Saturday in October, anyway—I knew this would be for us. Love, marriage, passion…a family together. I never doubted it…not for a moment, you know."

"I know," Talli whispered.

Still holding her face in his hands, Ruger gazed, oh, so very lovingly into her eyes. "This is us forever, you know, baby—being the happiest when we're with each other, facing life and laughing through it together, crying through it at times…but always together. Oh sure, we'll get old and fat, and I'll probably go bald."

"With this mane? Never," Talli said, reaching up to run her fingers through the sable of his hair.

"But we'll always laugh and love. We'll always know that we were meant to be together," he said in a lowered voice. "We'll always, always be together…even when we're dead. You know it too, don't you."

It was a statement—not a question.

"I do know it," Talli said, brushing a tear from her temple.

Ruger released her then, lovingly caressing her cheek with the back of his hand. He reached to where one of the plastic sandwich bags lay on the picnic table next to his burrito. Pulling a long strip of green chile from the bag, he popped it in his mouth, quickly chewing and swallowing it as he continued to smile at Talli.

"Are you ready for some heat, baby?" he asked, winking at her.

"Always," Talli giggled, knowing what was coming next.

Ruger leaned toward her again, pausing a moment, however. "We're really having a baby," he whispered. "You can feel it."

"Yes," Talli reassured him.

"Well, I for one am really glad that that first day we met and you saw me keeping my cell phone in my front pocket? I'm really glad you saw fit to begin preserving my—"

"Don't say it!" Talli giggled, putting a hand over Ruger's mouth.

But he pushed her hand away and finished, "My testicles."

"You are going to tell that story to our kids, aren't you?" Talli laughed.

"Of course. When they're old enough," Ruger affirmed with a wink. "Now come here, my little green chile seed. I'm hot and need to share."

Talli didn't care that she and Ruger missed singing the national anthem as the balloon with the American flag launched. She wasn't even aware of the cheers from the crowd as the rest of the dawn patrol went aloft, blinking like giant fireflies as they rose into the dark morning sky. All she knew was the heat of Ruger's kiss—the moist, hot, green-chile flavor of the kiss of the man she loved—of the father of her baby. In those early morning moments of an Albuquerque October, Talli's breath was taken away by not only the sweet, fluttering feeling in her tummy—the feeling of their baby moving—but also by the butterflies taking flight in her stomach as her husband's superlative kiss flawlessly conveyed the depth of his love to her—conveyed his boundless and never-ending love for her—deliciously—with its side of green chile.

Author's Note

Okay, I'll come right out and admit it—I wrote this quick little romance candy fix for myself! I needed something lighthearted, easy, and just plain lacking too much drama. Naturally, being that I love both the Albuquerque International Balloon Fiesta and green chile, I thought it would be fun to write a romance incorporating both. Oh, how I wish I could share the balloon fiesta with everyone! I wish everyone in all the world could have a chance to see what I see almost every morning during the autumn, and many mornings in early winter! The balloons really are so beautiful as they drift across the clear blue Albuquerque skies on cool, crisp mornings. My heart leaps with delight at the sight of them.

And as far as green chile is concerned—I love that too! The familiar and beloved aroma of green chile roasting outside grocery stores and farmer's markets is so soothing to me. It makes me smile every time as I inhale deep breaths of the scent that to me is the harbinger of autumn (even though green chile starts coming in and being roasted in August). In his book Food: A Love Story, Jim Gaffigan himself pays tribute to New Mexico's green chile—and I really think Jim gets it! And it is something you have to get, you know?

There are those out-of-towners who don't take to green chile like most of us native New Mexicans do, and that's okay. But to those of us who love it to the very tips of our toes—the unique flavor that is only green chile—it really does have addictive properties. One finds oneself starting out with a couple of tablespoons of green chile heaped on a green chile bacon cheeseburger and then asking the lady at the Lotaburger counter for an extra side of green chile. Sometimes when the green chile is too hot for my poor old tongue to handle, I just sit and sniff one of the little plastic containers they give you your side of green chile in—sniff and dream, remembering all those years that the heat of the chile didn't bother me too much and I could just lap it up like a thirsty dog at a water puddle, you know?

Yep, my tongue can't take it anymore—not the way I like it anyway. It happened about five years ago. One day I was at Sadie's eating my carne adovada, and man! I about went through the roof! When I got home, I actually looked at my tongue—and there, staring back at me in my own reflection, was my Auntie's tongue! I won't go into details, but my tongue had changed over the years and now was super sensitive to anything spicy. Oh, believe me, I fought it for years and years. But the discomfort I would go through for a month after indulging in even a little green chile became really miserable. Therefore, when I decided to write another book incorporating the balloon fiesta, I decided to include my love of green chile as well. Kind of like that phantom limb thing, you know? When someone loses a limb but they are still able to sense it there—even have the desire to scratch an itch they feel on the long lost limb. Well, that's how this book was for me and my tongue—a reminiscence of the tongue I once had that could down green chile like there was no tomorrow! (Heavy sigh.)

I'm not kidding, by the way, that there is nothing on earth like a piping hot breakfast burrito enjoyed at the AIBF (Albuquerque International Balloon Fiesta). Seriously! Our family doesn't even go directly to the field. We stop off at the breakfast burrito place right there as you come down to the end of the paved pathway leading from the parking lot to the field, order ourselves a breakfast burrito, and sometimes don't even find a place to sit to eat it. It doesn't matter if we can't see because of the early morning dark. It doesn't matter if we're shivering because we were too lazy to wear as many layers as we should have until it warms up. We just stand there in the dark munching our perfectly nummy soft flour tortilla wrapped around a mixture of scrambled eggs, fried sausage, green peppers, onions, cheddar cheese, even chunks of potatoes if you want, and lots of green chile, sipping hot chocolate while waiting for the dawn patrol to launch. Mmmm! The memories alone are making me salivate!

Now, enough about food (for now). Let's get to the part of this book that's really going to earn me some mean reviews—that being the speed with which Ruger and Talli realize they are meant to be together and begin falling in love. Many will say, "Poppycock! It can't happen in real life!" Others will say, "I just felt they needed a better reason to fall in love." And one or two will write to me and chew me out for charging too much for a novella, tell me the names of my characters are stupid, and that no one on earth could ever know the first time they talk to someone that they're going to fall madly in love with that person and spend eternity together. Well, most people don't decide they're meant for one another and decide to get married the very first day they meet. But there are a few who do! And there are even more who I believe have that premonitory sensation— something telling them that this person is going to make their life complete. Don't believe me? Well, guess what—I am one of those people!

Like Talli, the day I first set eyes on my own sexy burrito boy—actually, he'd be more of a sexy crawfish boy—I knew that he was the one for me! Of course, Kevin was so gorgeous, and I was so young, and the circumstances were so impossible that I very often doubted that it could really happen—but it did! I never once had a doubt that Kevin was the only man who could match me so well and make me as happy as I am. Not that life isn't a pain in the neck sometimes—but it's Kevin who gets me through all that, you know? Kevin who makes me laugh the most of anyone in the world, Kevin who I can't imagine life without—ever!

I also know three other people—wait, four—wait, five—who had the same experience. That being that they knew the minute they met or began communicating with one another that they were each other's "meant to be." I do not encourage everyone to look for that particular way of knowing who will make them happy. I'm just saying that it absolutely does happen! It's rare, admittedly. But it's real, and no one will ever convince me differently—because it's true!

In fact, I'll even go one further and tell you this. I have a friend of about forty years who went on a first date with a guy one New Year's Eve and got engaged to him on New Year's Day! How are they doing, you might ask? Well, thirty-plus years later, they're still going strong!

I know that there are many out there who have had love, even instant and wonderful forever-type love, and lost it for a number or reasons. Life, the influence of others, the world in general can slip in and pull two people apart. For so many of my friends who have endured this kind of excruciating heartache, I'm not going to lie and tell them it will get better or that they'll move on and all will be well.

Heartache and hurt leave deep wounds, some that scar over and some that I believe never completely heal. If you're one of the ones who have been hurt, had your heart ripped apart, and felt as if you couldn't live through it, I want you to know that this book is more for you than even for the rest of us—no matter what we're struggling with. This is a book that I want you to feel transported back in time through—back to when you were young, unscathed by hurt, hopeful, and in love! Those years were our most carefree, right? No matter how great we have it as adults or how rotten we have it, that first true love never leaves you; it is part of who you are. So I hope you allowed Romance with a Side of Green Chile to help you to escape for the short time it takes you to read it. Smile and know that no matter what, you deserve every happiness that Talli has and that someday, one way or the other, you'll know happiness again.

It was short, it was tasty, and Ruger was hot! And I'm grateful that you allow me these little novella vacations that I so desperately need at times. Thank you for everything you give to me, including that!

Meanwhile, until we meet again, here are a few little snippets— just for fun, as always!

Yours,
Marcia Lynn McClure

Snippet #1—As you might have guessed, I've always loved the hot air balloons of Albuquerque. And I've always made sure my kids were able to fall in love with them too. My daughter, Sandy, loves them as much as I do, and sometimes I wonder if part of the reason might be that her memories as a child are close to Talli's. I was pregnant with my second baby the first time Kevin and I woke little two-and-a-half-year-old Sandy before the crack of dawn, bundled her up pajamas and all (including her Lola Bunny slippers), and drove out to an area south of what is now Paseo Del Norte Boulevard in Albuquerque to watch the special shapes rodeo launch. I had lovingly packed a very nutritious breakfast of a cold cinnamon Pop-Tart, a Golden Delicious apple, and who knows what else and stuffed it into her My Little Pony lunchbox with her My Little Pony thermos filled with milk. Sandy sat on the closed trunk of our little Dodge Colt and had the time of her life watching the huge special shapes balloons inflate and drift overhead. Most other years when Sandy and then Mitch and then Trent were little, I'd bundle all the kids up, and we'd head down to my mom and dad's house in the North Valley of Albuquerque and watch the balloons launch and drift from there. It was the perfect place to balloon watch, being that the old launch site wasn't far from my parents' home. It was wonderful! And I cherish those memories as some of my most precious in life!

Snippet #2—Talli is named for a little girl I know and love who is also named Talli. Her mom and I jokingly call her Talkie—ever since the day the auto-correct on my phone auto-corrected Talli to Talkie. Her mom says that Talkie fits Talli perfectly!

Snippet #3—One of the BFFs I dedicated Romance with a Side of Green Chile to (Amy L.C.L.) actually introduced me to the wonder of not only bagels with cream cheese but also bagels with cream cheese topped with strips of roasted green chile! Mmmm! Thanks for the memorable and life-altering introduction, Amy!

Snippet #4—My first "boyfriend" (meaning we went steady for, like, ten days to two weeks) was a boy named S.C. He was sixteen and I was fourteen at the time, and to be honest, I really only started going with him because the guy I liked had gotten back together with his girlfriend, and S.C. was the guy's best friend, and he talked me into going out with S.C. (I still feel bad about that! A learning experience, and a necessary one for many reasons, but admittedly not my best moment.) Awhile after mine and S.C.'s relationship pooped out, he began working up at one of the malls in Albuquerque. He worked in the food court of the mall making something called funnel cake! Yep! That was the first time I'd ever had funnel cake—somewhere between autumn of 1979 and spring of 1981. It was S.C. who introduced me to funnel cake, and in my mind's eye, I can still see him in his funnel cake uniform. I do have more and happier funnel cake stories—my favorite involving two authors you may have heard of, Josie Kilpack and James Dashner, while we were all signing books at the county fair at Thanksgiving Point in Lehi, Utah, a stone's throw away from a funnel cake stand. But that's a story for another time. For now, I'll confess that my guilt over S.C. was nagging at me every time I typed "funnel cake" in this book. But I love funnel cake, so I made it through by imagining eating some at the balloon fiesta this year. (I still feel bad about S.C. though.)

Snippet #5—"Red or green?" That's the big question around these here parts! And yes, "both" is a very acceptable answer. My answer is always "green," of course. So just in case my dreams of you being able to attend the AIBF one day ever come true, remember this when the sexy guy at the breakfast burrito stand asks, "Red or green?" He's referencing what kind of chile you want on your burrito, red or green. FYI, green is usually hotter than red. That can be very helpful if you're like me and you're over fifty with a worn-out tongue.

Snippet #6—(You may recognize the flavor of this snippet from the Author's Note in One Classic Latin Lover, Please. But keep going; there's more to it for this book!) The year I was a freshman in high school, my friend Amy and I had signed up for the beginning guitar class. The class was taught by the music/choir teacher; we'll call him Mr. S. for reasons of anonymity. Well, there are a few things that made that class really special and fun. The first of those special and fun things was that Amy and I were in the same class (of course). The second of those special and fun things was the fact that poor Mr. S. was an alcoholic, and even though our class was at the beginning of the day, poor, dear Mr. S. usually spent the entire time in his office getting sloshed. He was a sweet, white-haired old guy who used to sing our school fight song in a beautiful, deep, booming voice at every assembly. He was, however, and very sadly, as I said, an alcoholic. But we all loved him and were just fine with the fact that we truly self-taught ourselves guitar for fifty minutes every morning. And Amy and I became quite adept guitarists. (I eventually took Flamenco guitar lessons for a while, and Flamenco became my favorite music to play!) Now, although free time to fiddle around on our instruments and teach ourselves how to play was awesome—and although the entire class loved Mr. S. so much that we weren't about to rat him out—those two special and fun things weren't even the best special and fun things, at least to me. The most specialist and funnest thing in the class for Amy and me was the gorgeous eye candy in the form one Joe C'de Baca, a stunningly handsome junior at our school. Joe already knew a bit about guitar playing, which was obvious by the fact that he played a fairly good rendition of "Dust in the Wind." I'm sure he took the class for an easy elective fill, you know? Anyway, to be honest, I felt that Joe's life was a bit sad. He was absent a lot, was kind of quiet, and never spoke to anybody much. But he was good-looking, that's for sure! In fact, I was really bummed when I got my yearbook at the end of that year to discover Joe must've been absent on school picture day, because his photo wasn't in the yearbook! So I don't even have a photograph of him to look back on; I have to go on pure memory. I do remember he had light-colored eyes—green, I believe—which was part of his striking appearance—you know, light-green eyes against that perfectly brown Hispanic heritage skin and dark, dark hair? Yep! He was a hottie! I can remember how delighted I'd get whenever he'd pass me in the hall, smile at me, and give me an Albuquerque chin-thrust greeting! Butterflies in my stomach, you know? Anywho, Amy and I got better and better on our guitars, and we began to perform publicly, singing and playing together here and there throughout our freshman year. Despairingly, however, after the beginning guitar class ended, I never saw Joe C'de Baca again. Sad, huh? But fear not! For as you now know, I've immortalized him here in this book—the grown-up version of him anyway. You know him as Ruger Villarreal!

Snippet #7—So you know how so many of my books have real-life inspiration, right? Well, Talli's first meeting with Ruger—the one where she biffs it on the pavement, scorpioning right there in front of him and scraping her chin? Yep! Inspired by something that happened to my good friend—shall we call her Trixie, for anonymity's sake? There she was—a tall, slender, gorgeous young woman of perhaps nineteen, attending college in Rexburg, Idaho…when the college was called Ricks College. Well, she had seen this guy that was totally hot, and I think she had a class with him. One day she decided she was really going to turn his head once and for all! So she dressed to the T that day—perfect hair, perfect makeup, favorite dress, sexy suntan pantyhose, and her highest '80s heels (complete with ankle straps, if I remember correctly). Wow! What a babe, right!? Well, as Trixie was coming down the stairs in one of the buildings, she sees Mr. Hottie with a Naughty Body coming up the same stairs. Thinking she'd never looked hotter, Dixie gracefully descended the stairs toward the hot guy of her dreams when—BOOM! Down she went, twisting her ankle and sliding down the stairs on her knees. As she tried to stand back up, the hot guy asked, "Are you all right?" Of course, Trixie slapped on a toothy smile and said, "Oh yeah! I'm fine!"—even as she struggled to stand, knees bleeding and pantyhose running like a full-on faucet. Trixie didn't scorpion in front of the hot guy she wanted to impress—but it was just as bad! And, sadly, great fodder for my imagination!

Snippet #8—Back in the early to mid-1990s, fabric paint was all the rage! All of us young moms embellished sweatshirt after sweatshirt with fabric paints, especially for our kids! All kids everywhere in America in had fabric-painted sweatshirts bulging out of their dresser drawers. Most kids had Christmas fabric-painted sweatshirts, Easter fabric-painted sweatshirts, and mine definitely had Halloween fabric-painted sweatshirts. Well, being that fabric paint was so much fun, us 1990s moms also embellished sweatshirts with fabric paints for our friends and ourselves. And one year, I made the most controversial fabric paint embellished sweatshirt in the state of New Mexico! Taking a black sweatshirt and my base beginning, I dribbled some dark red fabric paint up near the collar of the sweatshirt so that it looked like drops of blood. I then, daring woman that I was, wrote, Dracula sucks! in big red fabric-painted letters across the front. Ghastly for the time period, I assure you! Naturally, I wore a blood-red mock-turtleneck under the black sweatshirt to give the appearance that my neck was all bloody. You may be laughing now, but back in the mid-'90s, believe me, I got some very disapproving looks for wearing a shirt that had the word "sucks" on it—even if it was a funny pun! So, you see, Talli probably found my old Dracula sucks! sweatshirt in the rag bin out in the garage or something and figured it would do for frying funnel cake at the balloon fiesta! ·

Snippet #9—Wagner Farms down in Corrales (you remember Wagner's from The Time of Aspen Falls) really does sell sandwich-sized plastic bags full of just plain old roasted green chile! You just walk into their little café area, open their refrigerated section, pick out a baggie, have them ring you up, and cow down! Oh, how I love the flavor of green chile (in case you haven't guessed that yet). And although I can't just sit and eat straight green chile anymore because of my tongue issues, I sure do love the smell of it and do have a random spoonful of mild green chile now and again. It's the flavor I like most, after all. Mmmm!

Snippet #10—What color is your Coke? I know that New Mexicans aren't the only ones who identify their soda pop by color instead of brand name. But just in case you're from a state that uses brand names, the conversation between the funnel cake stand workers on what color of "Coke" they want is absolutely taken from real life around here!

Snippet #11—Ruger's career as a professional chainsaw wood-carver was meant to be! When my brain first started simmering on the details for Romance with a Side of Green Chile, my first instinct was to have Ruger's profession be that of a chainsaw carver. I wrote it down, but as I was telling Kevin about it, he frowned and asked, "A chainsaw carver? Could he make a good living at that?" Needless to say, a little moment of doubt entered my brain, and so I jotted down a couple of other career paths for Ruger. None of them fit him, however, so I went with my gut and decided to make him a professional chainsaw carver. Now, keep in mind that I'm a local Burqueño—meaning that I occasionally go to the balloon field for a mass ascension, especially when someone is visiting from out of town, but the balloons are my thing so I've never hung around the field for any of the other events. Imagine my surprise then when, as I'm looking up the 2016 schedule for the balloon fiesta, I find out that the Albuquerque International Balloon Fiesta holds professional chainsaw carving invitationals, raffles, and auctions almost every day of the fiesta! Freaking awesome, right?! So there you have it! I wasn't crazy in thinking Ruger was a chainsaw carver! I was spot on!

Snippet #12—Frito pie. Here is a history of Frito pie, courtesy of Wikipedia:

The exact origins of the frito pie (or tacos frios) is not completely clear. It is believed that it was created somewhere in Mexico and was popular at fiestas before it took off in other countries like the United States.

The oldest known recipe using Fritos brand corn chips with chili was published in Texas in 1949. The recipe may have been invented by Daisy Doolin, the founder's mother and the first person to use Fritos as an ingredient in cooking, or Mary Livingston, his executive secretary. The Frito-Lay company attributes the recipe to Nell Morris, who joined Frito-Lay in the 1950s and helped develop an official cookbook, which included the Frito pie.

Another story claims that true Frito pie originated only in the 1960s with Teresa Hernández, who worked at the F.W. Woolworth's lunch counter in Santa Fe, New Mexico. Her Frito pie used homemade red chili con carne with cheddar cheese and onions, and was served in the bag—which was thicker in the 1960s.[1]

Nowadays, the Frito pie I make (and the only kind I've ever made) is one of those "easy" meals. Dump some Frito corn chips in a bowl, ladle on some piping-hot canned Hormel chili with beans, dowse it with shredded cheddar cheese, smatter on a few tomatoes (and a little lettuce if you like the yucky stuff), and finish it off with a dollop of sour cream. Voilà! Frito pie!

Snippet #13—I really do worry about Kevin, my sons, and my son-in-law getting testicular cancer from carrying their cell phones in their front pockets. I try not to nag them too much about it—but sometimes I just can't stop myself!

Snippet #14—Dion's—a New Mexico favorite! And the time our Dion's order-taker nearly passed out while in the presence of my good-looking youngest son! Yes, it's true—even the girl at the order counter when Ruger and Talli hit Dion's for salad and pizza on their first official date is based on a real-life experience of mine—or rather my youngest son's. Trent wasn't quite twenty-one yet and had just returned home from being away for a couple of years when Kevin and I took him to fulfill his craving for a Dion's salad and pizza or specialty sandwich. As we approached the order counter, the young and very pretty girl's eyes widened to the size of Dion's courtesy

[1] Wikipedia contributors, "Frito pie," *Wikipedia, The Free Encyclopedia*, https://en.wikipedia.org/w/index.php?title=Frito_pie&oldid=767648303 (accessed March 2, 2017).

paper plates when she spied Trent! She was probably about seventeen and literally could not look away from him for a moment. Then it just got funny, or sad (whichever way you personally see it), when the poor girl started babbling on while trying to take our order. Our order was simple, and yet the girl couldn't seem to punch it into the computer correctly. At one point, she even said to Kevin, "I don't know what's wrong with me right now! It's like my blood pressure went up or something," as she glanced to Trent and began fanning herself with one hand. Eventually, she did get our very simple order punched into the computer. (I believe it took her four tries to get it right.) Once our order had been correctly punched in, Kevin, Trent, and I found a booth and sat down to wait for it to be ready. As we watched the poor, blushing, nervous seventeen-year-old with sudden high blood pressure hurry to a couple of other female employees and point out Trent to them as well, Kevin and I smiled with pride in our son's charisma and good looks. Our son Trent, on the other hand, remained totally clueless that it all had even happened! Humility (a.k.a. cluelessness that he's handsome) is part of his charm, after all.

Snippet #15—The earwig in the drinking straw story—true, true, horribly true! It happened to my friend Kathy H. She always kept a glass of water on her nightstand next to her bed. One night she reached over, picked up her glass, and began to take a swig when she felt something crawling on her lip. Flipping on the light—SPIDER in her CUP!!!!! Ahhhhh! Don't get me started on whether the spider was already on her or in her cup—all that nonsense about us all eating spiders in our sleep entirely freaks me out, even though I know it's an urban myth! However, Kathy says she was sure the spider was in her cup. Needing water at night and not wanting to risk another spider encounter, Kathy purchased a water bottle with a sturdy straw included. The first night she had the water bottle, Kathy drifted off to sleep on the wings of peace in knowing no spider would wander into her glass of water during the night, right? So in the middle of the night, Kathy wakes up thirsty. Remembering that she now has the spider-proof water bottle with accompanying sturdy straw, she takes a big swig of water—yet instantly she realizes something is amiss. Flipping on the light and racing to the bathroom sink, Kathy spit the water into the sink only to find…EARWIG!!!! Apparently an earwig had squiggled down into her straw during the night! Ugh! As for me, I just keep a regular water bottle on my nightstand now—lid screwed on tight so nothing can wriggle in when I'm not looking! Yuck!

Snippet #16—There's a little movie our family enjoyed for years—She's the Man. Well, there's a little quote from that movie that both of my sons used to use—rather, I'd tell both of my sons to think it—when they were in high school and feeling like they were never going to be finished with dealing with people who weren't their choice to deal with. "Screw you guys! I hate high school!" Yes, both of my boys made it through high school using this mantra and knowing that, one day, they wouldn't have to deal with high school ever again. (Now, that's seriously a trivial snippet, right?)

Snippet #17—The first time Kevin ever showed me a photograph of one of his sisters, I nearly dropped dead with feeling inadequate! It was a senior picture of his younger sister, Kristi, who was a year younger than me. My feelings at the sight of how gorgeous she was (which makes sense, being that Kevin is so gorgeous) were the same as Talli's when she first sees Kimber. I really didn't know how in the world I was going to exist in a family of such beautiful people! So that is another way that I totally relate to Talli's insecurities.

Snippet #18—Ruger and Talli's song, "Run to Me," is definitely an oldie! It has been recorded by tons of artists along the way, but my favorite version is the one by the Bee Gees, who also composed the song. Why then did it end up being Ruger and Talli's song? Because when Ruger is trying to reassure Talli of the truth of their budding relationship's being real, the song just popped into my head! Plus, Barry Gibb really did have lovely hair back in the day, you know?

Snippet #19—Sprouting warts. Yep. It's a phrase coined by my youngest son. I think he was in third grade. As always, I was picking him up from school. He plopped into the front seat of the car and exhaled a heavy sigh.

"How was your day?" I asked.

"Okay. But we had a sub," my son answered.

"Oh no! Was Mrs. Lucas (his teacher) absent again?" I inquired (being that his teacher seemed to be absent a lot.)

"Yeah," he sighed.

"What's wrong with her?" I inquired.

"Oh, I don't know," he grumbled with great irritation. "She has some disease where if she goes out in the sun she sprouts warts or something."

I just want to say that it was often a good thing that I didn't start the car right away when my kids got in after school—especially when my youngest did. Because as serious as he was being, I nearly experienced incontinence issues with that particular response. The term "sprouts warts" has stuck with me ever since.

(I want to emphasize that neither one of us finds any sort of pain, disease, or illness humorous. It was just his wording that has stuck with me all these years as so incredibly amusing!)

Snippet #19—The Sandia crest is a really popular place for marriage proposals. The fastest way to get there is to ride the tram up, and even though the restaurant that used to be up at the top of the crest is being remodeled right now, I'm sure it will continue to be a big "dinner and proposal" spot for local Albuquerque residents for a long, long time to come. In fact, the last time Kevin and I were up there, we saw a guy and girl who were obviously up there for the proposal reason. How did we know? The guy was decked out in a fancy-shmancy suit and the poor girl was wearing one of those wide pieces of elastic that serves as a dress and seven-inch heels! It was kind of sad, because the temperature at the top of the crest where the tram lets you off is always a million degrees lower than it is in the foothills where you hop on it. So needless to say, the poor girl was freezing her piece of elastic off! Still, the guy managed to propose and get someone to snap a picture before they hopped back on the tram to head down to the warmer climate. You might be thinking that maybe the guy should've given his girlfriend a heads up that they were going to the crest. Well, my guess is that he did! Most native Burqueños are so used to our moderate weather that they don't even own a heavy coat!

Snippet #20—Here's a little cooking tip: if you want to try some canned green chile that has the true New Mexico flavor, purchase only the Hatch brand of green chile at your supermarket! Hatch is the best green chile anyway, and somehow their canned green chile manages to hold onto its flavor the best when canned.

To my hero and inspiration...
Kevin from Heaven!

About the Author

Marcia Lynn McClure's intoxicating succession of novels, novellas, and e-books—including Shackles of Honor, The Windswept Flame, A Crimson Frost, and The Bewitching of Amoretta Ipswich—has established her as one of the most favored and engaging authors of true romance. Her unprecedented forte in weaving captivating stories of western, medieval, regency, and contemporary amour void of brusque intimacy has earned her the title "The Queen of Kissing."

Marcia, who was born in Albuquerque, New Mexico, has spent her life intrigued with people, history, love, and romance. A wife, mother, grandmother, family historian, poet, and author, Marcia Lynn McClure spins her tales of splendor for the sake of offering respite through the beauty, mirth, and delight of a worthwhile and wonderful story.

BIBLIOGRAPHY

A Bargained-For Bride
Beneath the Honeysuckle Vine
A Better Reason to Fall in Love
The Bewitching of Amoretta Ipswich
Born for Thorton's Sake
The Chimney Sweep Charm
Christmas Kisses-Three Favorite Holiday Romances
A Cowboy for Christmas
A Crimson Frost
Daydreams
Desert Fire
Divine Deception
Dusty Britches
The Fragrance of her Name
A Good-Lookin' Man
The Haunting of Autumn Lake
The Heavenly Surrender
The Highwayman of Tanglewood
Kiss in the Dark
Kissing Cousins
The Light of the Lovers' Moon
Love Me
The Man of Her Dreams
The McCall Trilogy
Midnight Masquerade
The Object of His Affection
An Old-Fashioned Romance
One Classic Latin Lover, Please

The Pirate Ruse
The Prairie Prince
The Rogue Knight
Romance at the Christmas Tree Lot
Romance in Sleepy Hollow
The Romancing of Evangeline Ipswich
Romantic Vignettes-The Anthology of Premiere Novellas
Romance with a Side of Green Chile
Saphyre Snow
Shackles of Honor
The Secret Bliss of Calliope Ipswich
The Stone-Cold Heart of Valentine Briscoe
Sudden Storms
Sweet Cherry Ray
Take a Walk with Me
The Tide of the Mermaid Tears
The Time of Aspen Falls
To Echo the Past
The Touch of Sage
The Trove of the Passion Room
Untethered
The Visions of Ransom Lake
Weathered Too Young
The Whispered Kiss
With a Dreamboat in a Hammock
The Windswept Flame
The Wolf King

CPSIA information can be obtained
at www.ICGtesting.com
Printed in the USA
FSOW02n0740230517
34432FS